I0836352

Van Gogh's Show

THE FORGOTTEN EXHIBITION

Impressionists of the Petits Boulevards

SHORT HISTORY AND NOVELLA

RL Foster

Innovative Books
2019

Van Gogh's Show

By RL Foster

Wilmington, North Carolina
info@innovativebooks.net

Introduction

Human convergences have always fascinated me. My art gallery was such a place. At the gallery's grand opening. Two women friends attended with their husbands. In the course of the evening, each was to encounter an old spouse who they had not seen in decades. One woman was even approached by her ex-husband who didn't even recognize her from twenty years ago. For the ten years of the gallery's existence, these kinds of odd human reconnections were continuing occurrences.

Van Gogh's Show is a fictional account of another opening. In late November 1887, Vincent Van Gogh organized a Paris exhibit and gave it the name, *Les Impressionnistes des Petits Boulevards*—The Impressionists of the Small Boulevards. The show was to present the art of the emerging artists whom did not show at the galleries on the grand boulevards where the major artists such as Renoir and Degas showed. Before writing this short history and novella, I included the exhibition in a scene in my play, *A Short Evening with Toulouse Lautrec*. The artists in the play and the book were those who painted with Van Gogh at the Fernand Cormon atelier. The most famous was Henri Toulouse-Lautrec, but Emile Bernard and Louis Anquetin would also experience some short-lived fame.

I pondered who else may have attended the opening of

the show. There's no account of that evening but I came up with a potential cast of intriguing characters—all of them would find some place in art history and beyond. The Paris art community was tight-knit and would have attracted Suzanne Valadon, who modeled for a few of Lautrec's paintings. Paul Gauguin had just returned to Paris and was a friend of both Bernard and Anquetin. Misia Godebska (Natanson, Sert) was giving piano lessons in the city while Walter Sickert and James Whistler were regular Paris visitors and both would become friends of Lautrec.

I was tempted to indulge in further research to see where the characters were in that last week of November. As a writer, I would prefer to simply make the assumption that they all were there. Of course, one might say as a fiction writer it would not have made any difference of their whereabouts. But the process of writing is much more pleasurable when the narrative has a feeling of truth. If I had discovered that one or more of the characters were not there, I probably would have chosen to omit them and they all needed to be in the story. So did the evening unfold as written? If something cannot be disproved, then all is possible.

The Exhibition

Impressionists of the Petits Boulevards was the name coined by Vincent Van Gogh for the Paris exhibition he organized in November of 1887. Petits boulevards was Van Gogh's term to separate this work from that of the more renowned Impressionists, such as Monet and Renoir whose paintings were exhibited at the more prestigious galleries of the *grands boulevards*. The exhibit was largely ignored by the French press and we don't know whether the exhibition was formally titled.

Perhaps, the most remarkable aspect of the exhibition was that it was organized by Van Gogh, who was viewed then, as he is today, as a social maladroit. From the very beginning, the exhibition was marked by personal antagonisms. Van Gogh originally intended to invite all of his "friends" to participate, but they were clustered into two different artistic factions: the Pointillists or Divisionists led by Georges Seurat and Paul Signac and the Synthesists or Cloisonnists led by Emile Bernard and Louis Anquetin. Seurat's painting A Sunday Afternoon in the Island of La Grande is the most famous Pointillist painting whereas

Bernard's, *Bathers with Red Cow* exemplifies the Synthetist style.

Ultimately, the Pointillists refused to show with the others, and only Van Gogh, Bernard, Anquetin, Henri Toulouse-Lautrec and Van Gogh's amateur friend Arnold Koening were in the show.

Van Gogh convinced the owner of a restaurant where he took lunch to allow him to exhibit in a recently closed ballroom above the restaurant. Le Grand Bouillon Restaurant du Chalet at 43 Avenue de Cliche was a working-class.The ballroom itself was ideally suited for an exhibition with high bay windows that generously lit the room. Little is known about the actual logistics of the exhibition, but we can assume that Theo Van Gogh, Vincent's brother, would have assisted in the setup of the show.

All of the artists, except for Koning, had painted together at Fernand Cormon's atelier, which had recently closed as a rebellion against Cormon's classical orientation. At thirty-four, Van Gogh was the oldest painter while Lautrec had just turned twenty-three and Bernard was only nineteen. None of the artists had established great reputations at the time, but they were familiar figures in the Parisian avant-garde art community. Impressionism was a term that was loosely thrown around at the time. Indeed, none of the artists with the ironic exception of Koenig were true Impressionists, and probably did not view themselves as such.

These artists would have starved if they had to depend on art sales for their livelihood. Except for Van Gogh they all came from affluent families. If he had survived his father, Lautrec would have been Count Toulouse-Lautrec. Bernard and Anquetin were single children from well-to-do bourgeoisie families. It has been claimed that Van Gogh only sold one painting in his lifetime. This is probably a popular myth, but indeed, he would not have survived as an artist if it was not for the assistance of his devoted brother Theo, who was a successful Paris art dealer.

The show received no attention from the popular press, and there is little indication that it kindled much of a public response. There was certainly no money available for promotion, and the artists were virtual unknowns to the general public. However, the avant-garde Parisian art community was tight-knit and the exhibition would have attracted their attention. Without collector support, it was not surprising that sales were almost non-existent.

We have little information on what paintings were displayed at the exhibit. There is some indication that Toulouse- autrec showed several of his female figurative works. His two paintings of Suzanne Valadon, *Rice Power* and *The Hangover* were probably included. Bernard had just begun experimenting with his Synthetist style and we would have expected samples of this work such as *Bathers with Red Cow* and *Young Woman in Kimono* were probably included in the show. Van Gogh painted a diversity of work in Paris in 1887 and it is reasonable to assume the show included a few Paris street scenes, some still lifes and perhaps a few female figures. Louis Anquetin, the least prolific of the group, probably exhibited his *Avenue de*

Clichy work, showing the influence of the Synthetist concepts.

Not only was the exhibit ignored by the press and the general public, there appears to have not been a great deal of flutter among the artists themselves. Bernard casually mentions the show in some of his correspondence, but the voluminous letter-writer, Toulouse-Lautrec does not mention the exhibition in any of his letters to his family. Van Gogh makes casual allusions to it in 1888, but nothing of substance. It appears it was a show that everyone wanted to forget, and its financial failure was probably one of the reasons that Van Gogh decided to leave Paris the following year.

The exhibit was prematurely closed by the end of the year because of complaints the restaurant owner received from his patrons who were annoyed by the continual stream of artists who came to see the show. No one seemed particularly disappointed by its quick demise.

Historically, the exhibit has not been considered one of significance. Probably much of this ignoring can be attributed to the infinitesimal amount of information we have regarding the exhibition. In many ways this is disappointing; Van Gogh was approaching the height of his creative powers with his later dementia still in abeyance. He would be dead in less than three years.

Toulouse-Lautrec was just coming into his own as a unique creative talent. His paintings in this exhibit were a progression from his traditional leanings and included some of his finest oil paintings.

Although the Synthetist art movement was minor and short-lived, it was probably the first time such paintings were exhibited in the works of Bernard and Anquetin. Paul Gauguin was in Paris at the time, and was friendly with both Bernard and Anquetin, so we would have to believe he attended the show. At the time, his style was moving toward Synthetism, and the show would have reinforced this direction. We would also believe that Suzanne Valadon visited the exhibition since she modeled for several of Toulouse- Lautrec's paintings. She would eventually carve out her own reputation as an important Expressionist with work that would show many leanings from Bernard's and Anquetin's paintings.

Impressionists of the Petits Boulevards was little more than a glint on Paris's artistic horizon. Although hardly recognized then and now, it was the confluence of some of modern art's most enigmatic and iconic personalities whose lives would branch in very different directions.

The Players

Vincent Van Gogh

Henri Toulouse-Lautrec

Louis Anquetin

Emile Bernard

Paul Gauguin

Suzanne Valadon

Misia Godebska (Natanson/Sert)

Walter Sickert

James Whistler

Vincent Van Gogh

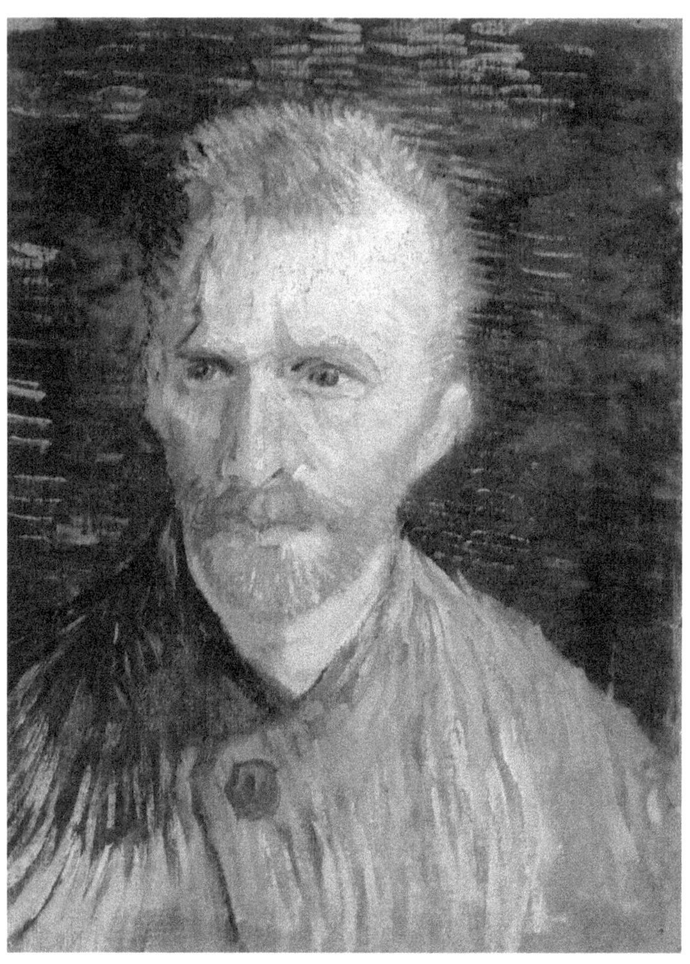

Self Portrait (1887)
Vincent Van Gogh
Oil on canvas, 18 x 13.5"

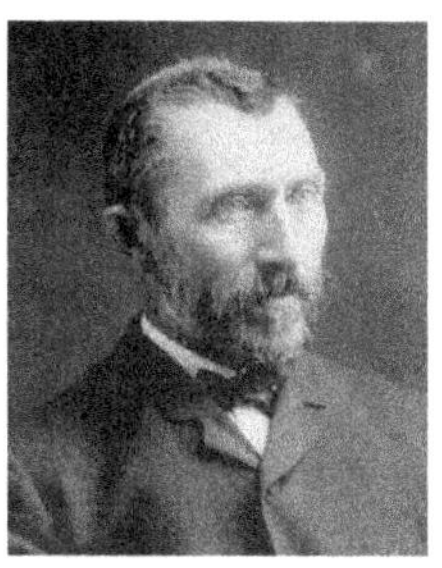

Vincent Van Gogh

"I put my heart and my soul into my work, and have lost my mind in the process."

Vincent Van Gogh arrived in Paris in 1886 at the age of thirty-three. Paris was the art center of Europe, and Van Gogh came hoping to make his mark as an important artist. Up to this point in his life, he had failed in virtually every endeavor he attempted—first, as an art dealer and later as a Christian missionary.

He was a loner and no doubt already suffered from some personality disorder. He had few friends and if it weren't for the fanatical devotion of his brother Theo, he would have been utterly alone. The longest romantic attachment he had been able to sustain was with a Dutch prostitute, whom he ultimately abandoned after six months.

At thirty-three, he already looked twenty years older. He had a meager existence, and with what money he did receive, he was more likely to spend it on paint, canvas and drink rather than food. He had developed a fondness for absinthe and was probably an alcoholic. His personal grooming was almost non-existent, and his clothes reeked with the stench of tobacco. All of his self-portraits at this time show a gaunt man with a wizened face and sharp features. Lautrec's crayon portrait of him depicts a driven personality with an uncomfortable intensity.

Although he had some formal training, he believed that Paris would be an opportunity to expand his abilities. His brother enrolled him in Fernand Cormon's atelier which was devoted to classical training. He was older than the other painters, the only non-French artist, and was viewed as a quirky outsider. Much of any acceptance that he might have had depended on the position of his brother, who was an active and successful Paris art dealer. At Cormon's, he painted with several artists who would leave their mark on art history, including Toulouse-Lautrec and Emile Bernard. Through Bernard and Louis Anquetin, he would be introduced to Paul Gauguin which would evolve into a tragic friendship.

Van Gogh was seldom included in Lautrec's nightly led escapades in Montmartre, a popular theatrical and art area of Paris. He did show up for Lautrec's weekly soirées, which were punctuated by lively conversations regarding art and life in general. Van Gogh had little interest in these conversations and rarely participated. He preferred instead to unfurl his most recent canvas with the hope of generating interest among the group, which rarely occurred. Frustrated by this lack of attention, he would roll up the canvas and leave in an angry huff.

How this hermitic misanthrope could have organized *Les Petits Boulevards* is certainly something of a mystery.

No doubt he envisioned an exhibition of grander scale with Pointillist work of Pissarro, Seurat, and Signac who were all initially invited to participate. They latter declined because of a dispute with Bernard and Anquetin having had recently abandoned Pointillism for a new art style they called Cloisonnism which would be later referred to as Synthetism. The exhibit opened in November of 1887 with no catalog or presses to support it. Without this support, the show drew little public attention, but was attended by many of the Parisian art community, especially the younger avant-garde artists. Surprisingly, so many artists attended, that it caused complaints from the restaurant's lunch patrons who were disturbed by the continual flow of artists who had to traipse through the restaurant to get to the ballroom upstairs where the exhibit was held. This led to a dispute between the restaurant owner and Van Gogh resulting in the show being abruptly withdrawn in less than a month.

What paintings of his own that Van Gogh included in the show is not exactly known. He was very prolific during the year, painting a diversity of subject matters. Ironically, one of his favorite subjects during this time was himself, but self-portraits of a little-known painter would hardly attract sales attention so the assumption would be that the work would have focused on the human and cityscape elements of Montmartre where he lived and painted. None of his paintings sold although he might have traded some with the artists.

Les Petits ushered in his artistic brilliance and the beginning of his descent into madness. His interaction with the Impressionists had significantly brightened his palette. In fact, he thought of himself as a colorist, and viewed color as a dominant attribute of modern painting. He remarked, "The painter of the future will be a colorist such as never yet existed." No doubt, he saw himself as that painter. Like most of his young avant-garde compatriots, he collected and appreciated Asian woodblock prints. Many of these decorative principles found their way into his art. He also began to explore and refine his stylized brushstrokes that would come to dominate his work in his final years.

After *Les Petits*, Van Gogh would leave Paris, never to return. He had invited Gauguin to join him in Arles where he envisioned an art colony headed by he and Gauguin. Apparently, Gauguin was not excited by the prospect and repeatedly postponed the trip. After weeks of badgering, Gauguin finally arrived to join Van Gogh in his small two-bedded house. Initially, the reunion was happy with the two painting Arles landscapes and visiting the local galleries. Their honeymoon quickly darkened as Van Gogh resented egocentric displays of superiority.

Van Gogh's jealousy grew when Gauguin began spending his evenings drinking and convorting at the local cafe. His jealousy came to a head when Van Gogh followed Gauguin as he departed the nightly cafe visit. Gauguin wasn't concerned until he noticed that Van Gogh was brandishing a razor. Van Gogh angrily returned to his house after the confrontation. Gauguin decided prudently that he should spend the night in a hotel.

Van Gogh returned to the yellow house so enraged that

he cut off his ear and returned to the cafe in search of Garguin. Not finding him, he presented the ear to a cafe cleaning girl who apparently informed the police

The next day the police found Van Gogh unconscious and took him to the hospital where he was treated by treated by Doctor Félix Rey. Rey would treat his Van Gogh for his remaining days and would be the subject of one of Van Gogh's painting. Dr. Rey had little fondness for the painting and supposedly used it to repair a chicken coup before giving it away. The painting is now in the Pushkin Museum in Moscow where it is valued at $50 million.

Van Gogh was ordered to a hospital for acute mania and Gauguin quickly left after informing Theo Van Gogh of his brother's condition.

Van Gogh eventually recovered from this episode but mental illness plagued him for the rest of his life. Despite multiple hospitalizations and incapacitations in Arles, it may have been the most productive period in his life. He produced hundreds of works including some of his greatest and most memorable paintings.

Van Gogh's mental condition continued to disintegrate in and he was forced to leave Arles and enter an asylum in Saint-Rémy, about 20 miles from Arles. He was provided two cells with bars—one for living and one for painting. In moments of lucidity, he completed some of his greatest masterpieces, including *The Starry Night.*

He recovered enough to leave Saint-Rémy and to be closer to his new doctor Paul Gachet in the Paris suburb of Auvers-sur-Oise.

Initally he was invigorated by the golden wheat fields that surrounded him, but his depression grew and with it his will to paint. On 27 July 1890,Van Gogh shot himself in the wheat field where he had been painting. He hung on for a few days, but died with his brother Theo at his side.

He was buried July 30, 1890 in the municipal cemetery of Auvers-sur-Oise. Of the artists of *Impressionists of the Petits Boulevards*, only Emile Bernard attended.

Woman in the Cafe Tambourin, (1887)
Vincent Van Gogh, Oil on canvas, 22 × 19”

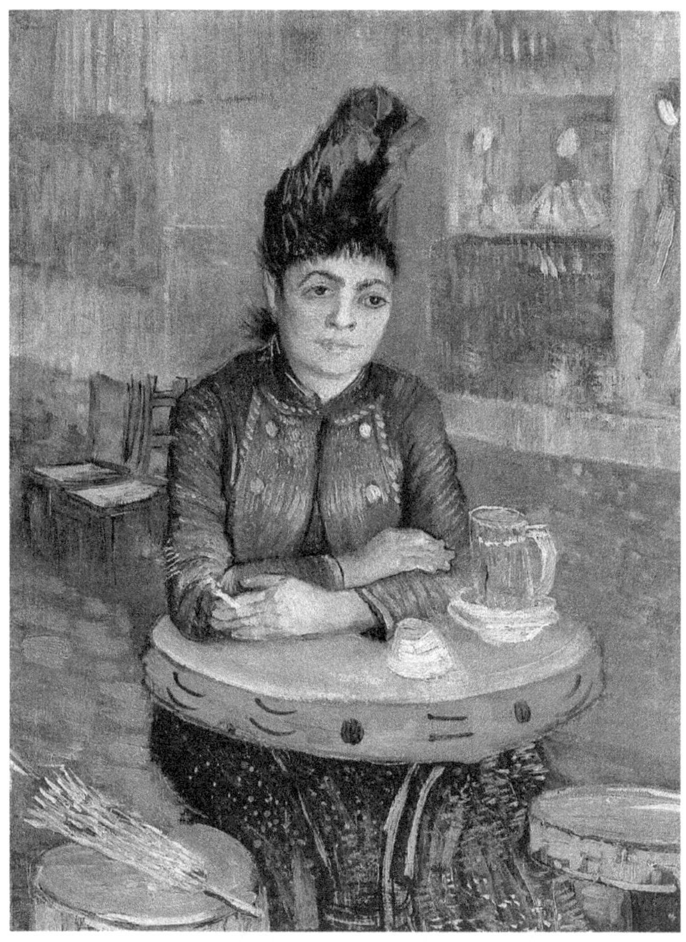

PAINTING: The model for the painting was Agostina Segatori who was the owner of the Café du Tambourin. Van Gogh had organized an exhibition at the café to sell his collection of Japanese prints. Some of the prints can be seen in the background of this portrait. He may have painted Agostina during the exhibition.

Henri Toulouse-Lautrec

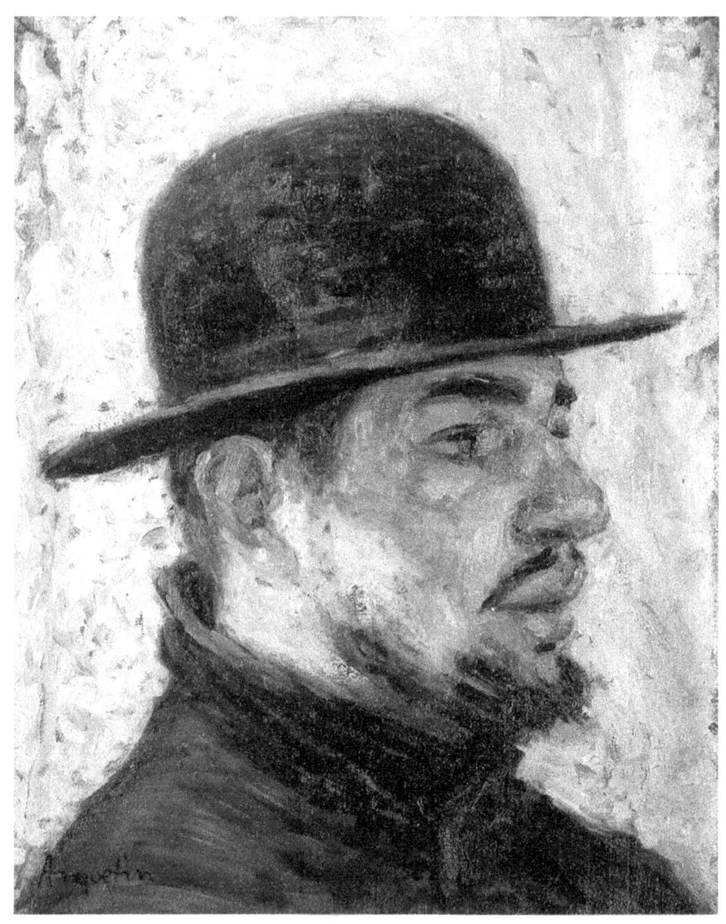

Henri Toulouse-Lautrec (1886)
Louis Anquetin
Oil on canvas, 16 x 13"

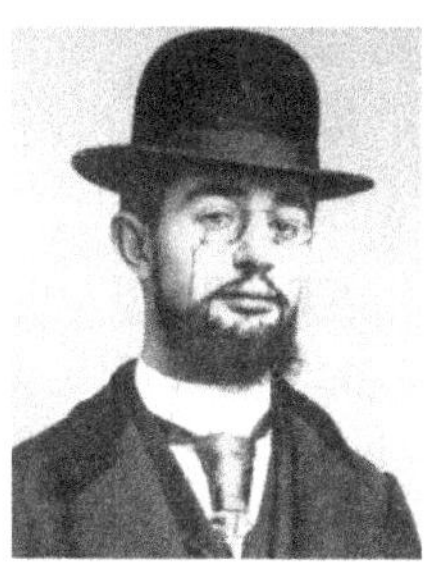

Henri Toulouse-Lautrec

"I paint things as they are. I don't comment"

Henri Toulouse-Lautrec had just turned twenty-three the day before the opening of the Les Petits Boulevards. The evening was to serve as celebration for both his birthday and the opening of the exhibition. If he had outlived his father, he would have become Count Toulouse-Lautrec. Although he maintained a sardonic view of his heritage, at his core, he was a patrician, who loved his family.

When he was sixteen, Lautrec had come to Paris to become an artist. His family had ambivalent feelings regarding his decision. In the end, Lautrec's obvious artistic skills swung the decision in his favor. The hope was that he could become a society portrait painter, and he was enrolled in the atelier of Léon Bonnat, a well-known academic portrait painter.

His choice of career was met by disdain by his family, especially his father, who thought that any career was beneath the noble class. Much of Lautrec's emotional energy was directed to winning favor with his father. There is no evidence that he succeeded, and Lautrec would bemoan the lack of financial support from his family.

Much has been made of Lautrec's grotesqueness. Except for his misshapen and dwarfed legs, he was not unattractive. He had a well-proportioned face with full lips and a strong nose. His most striking feature was his penetrating gray eyes beneath a set of dark, long eyebrows. He was only four and a half feet tall, but his torso was that of a normal man while his legs were half the normal size. It appeared that he must have suffered from a genetic disease that his family's rampant inbreeding contributed greatly. The true nature of his disease is uncertain, but modern medical experts believe he suffered from pycnodysostosis, a form of dwarfism. Today, it is also called "Toulouse-Lautrec's disease." Even as a young man he required the assistance of a cane. Besides the skeletal issues, he was continually subjected to multiple maladies from chronic bronchial problems to a persistent nasal drip.

Despite these challenges, he was an animated young man, who delighted in playing tricks on his friends. He had a puckish quality that his friends found endearing. For the most part, he had a good-natured disposition, but he was not the kind of person you wanted to cross. The jokes he played on friends could often approach meanness, and if you were the target of his animus they were often cruel.

Although he was smart and quick-witted, he was not a deep thinker; nor was he particularly innovative in his intellectual disposition. His emergence into the new avant-garde Parisian scene, was founded more on a desire to be accepted by his young peer artists who dismissed the traditional Salon artists as passé and moribund. Among his friends, he was leader in their nocturnal escapades to the clubs and bistros of Montmartre, an area in Paris dominated by creative and theater types.

He was involved with the promiscuous model Suzanne Valadon, and two of his paintings of her were no doubt included in the exhibit. The two barroom scenes, *Rice Powder* and *The Hangover*, show a moody model, who appears bored by the moment and perhaps wishing to be elsewhere.

Valadon was only twenty-three at the time but already had become a favorite model of some of Paris's most prominent artists including Degas and Renoir. She had aspirations herself to become an artist and Lautrec was one of the few artists she would show her work. Valadon's ego would have guaranteed her presence at the opening of the show.

Valadon was a fiery companion who would shortly leave the relationship with Lautrec and ultimately would become a significant artist in her own right.

Lautrec would also develop a platonic relationship with Misia Godebska (Natanson/Sert), the young artistic patron of the Parisian avant-garde scene. Although she was only fifteen at the time, she was supporting herself as a piano teacher and was sophisticated beyond her years. It is not beyond the realm of possibility that she could have met Lautrec at this opening. Lautrec would paint a famous portrait of her at the piano some ten years later.

At the time of *Le Petits*, he was still a relative unknown in the Parisian art society, but over the next two decades, he would become one of the era's most well-known art celebrities. His paintings have not received the same level of fame as Van Gogh's, but his lithographs are widely recognized as some of the finest ever produced. Despite his noble ancestry, Lautrec was always in need of money. The allowance from his mother and father was hardly sufficient to support his Paris lifestyle. He did not paint portrait commissions and his art sales were always marginal. His income from lithographs and book covers made up for the small allowance he received from the family.

Lautrec's life was challenged by poor health, and the excesses of drinking and prostitutes caused his death from the complications of alcholism amd syphilis in 1901 at the age of thirty-six. He was buried in Cimetière de Verdelais, near his mother's estate. No artists were invited.

Rice Powder (1887)
Henri Toulouse-Lautrec, Oil on canvas, 22 × 18”

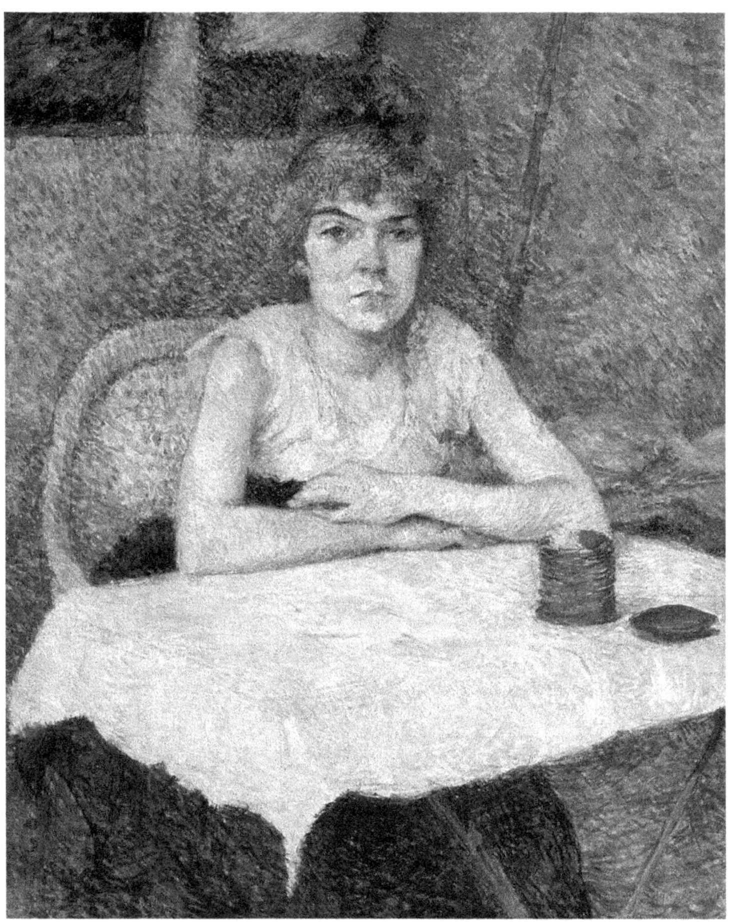

PAINTING: Before their testy rupture, Suzanne Valadon was a favorite Lautrec model. She would move on Edgar Degas who befriended and tutored her,

Louis Anquetin

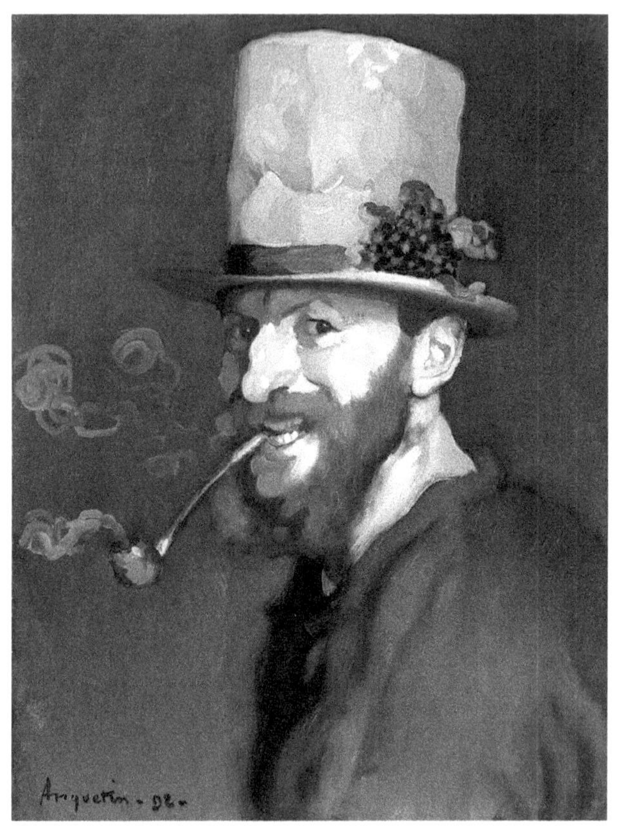

Self Portrait (1886)
Louis Anquetin
Oil on canvas, 25.7 x 19.4"

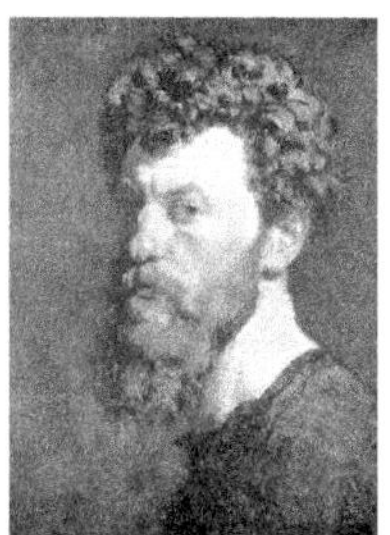

Louis Anquetin

"With Rubens I discovered my love of art."

Louis Anquetin was twenty-six when Les Petits opened. In the Parisian art scene, he was viewed as one of its brightest stars. He was regarded in much higher esteem than any of the other painters in the exhibit including Van Gogh and Toulouse-Lautrec. He was a compatriot of Lautrec's nightly revels through Montmartre, and was Emile Bernard's intellectual partner in the development of the artistic movement called Synthetism and the related movement, *Cloisonnism.*

Anquetin was the only child of an affluent bourgeois butcher. He convinced his parents early-on to support his decision to become an artist. He was enrolled at the Lycee Pierre Corneille in Rouen at the age of eleven, and in 1880 he graduated. After spending two years in the French Dragoons, he returned to Paris. He enrolled in the atelier of Léon Bonnat where he met and became friends with Lautrec. Two years later, both he and Lautrec joined the atelier of Fernand Cormon where they would meet Van Gogh and Emile Bernard.

Like many of the young Parisian painters, he would spend part of his summers at Pont-Aven, a quaint Brittany village, which had become a summer Mecca for artists. It was here that he and Emile Bernard began exploring new art potentials that would evolve into Synthetism. The pair would have no doubt encountered Paul Gauguin who was also a regular visitor.

Anquetin was a tall, handsome man with elegant manners. Like Lautrec, he was very much a social animal, and they must have made a strange pair for Anquetin stood well over six feet while dwarfish Lautrec was well under five feet. Of all the Les Petits artists, Anquetin was the most socially adept and flexible in his life. He was prone to experimentation and painted in many styles. He would eventually embrace a classical style. He and Bernard initially delved into a form of Impressionism called *Divisionism* or *Pointillism*, which was advanced by Georges Seurat and Paul Signac. This attraction was short-lived, and they went on to develop a style they called *Cloisonnism*, which was later to be known as *Synthetism*, a forerunner of 20th Century Expressionism. For a brief period, he even produced work reminiscent of Lautrec's lithographic style.

Like Bernard, he had begun experimenting with this new Synthetist style when Les Petits opened. Unlike Van Gogh and Lautrec whose sole passion was painting, Anquetin was involved in other intellectual pursuits, and was much less prolific in his output of artwork. No doubt his Avenue de Clinchy: Five O'Clock in the Evening was included in the show. The early evening city scene would become one of his most recognizable works and it has been suggested that it inspired Van Gogh's famous *Cafe Terrace at Night*, which was painted the following year. There is no evidence that any of his paintings sold including *Avenue de Clinchy*, which found its way into two exhibitions in 1888. Other pieces in the show might have included an oil painting, At the Circus, a subject matter popularized by Lautrec.

After *Les Petits*, Anquetin continued to paint Synthetist pieces for the next decade. He participated in the 1889 Volpini exhibition with Paul Gauguin and Bernard and contributed seven paintings. The show was organized by Gauguin and was supported with a poster and an illustrated catalog. Unfortunately, the show was received with the same lack of public enthusiasm as the *Les Petits exhibition*.

Anquetin enjoyed some renown for his Synthetist work, but like Bernard did not receive the same recognition as Gauguin, who became identified with the Synthetist style despite usurping the recognition from Bernard and Anquetin. Gradually he moved away from Synthetism to a more classical style and would later totally reject modernism. This disavowal alienated him from most of his former comrades. Only Lautrec, who avoided allegiances to any artistic ideology, remained friends.

During a 1894 trip to Belgium with Toulouse-Lautrec, he was exposed to the Northern Baroque art of Rembrandt, Franz Hals, and particularly Peter Paul Rubens whose style and art he greatly admired. He proclaimed the importance of proper anatomy. From 1894 to 1896, he studied anatomy in the laboratory of Professor Arroux in Clamart as he believed that great classical painters had mastered the perfect knowledge of anatomy, which gave them the freedom of painting figures without relying on models. He also started experimenting with oil techniques trying to uncover the methods of the old masters. Later, as an academic, he would write a book on Rubens.

In 1906 he married a rich widow and retired from active painting. For the last 25 years of his life, he taught classical painting techniques in Paris. His contribution to post-modern art has been largely ignored and he died in near total obscurity in 1932. A few months before his death, he was visited by Bernard who painted a final tribute portrait of his old friend with the inscription, "Louis Anquetin, a token of my deepest admiration.

Avenue de Clinchy (1887)
Louis Anquetin, Oil on canvas, 27.2 × 20.9”

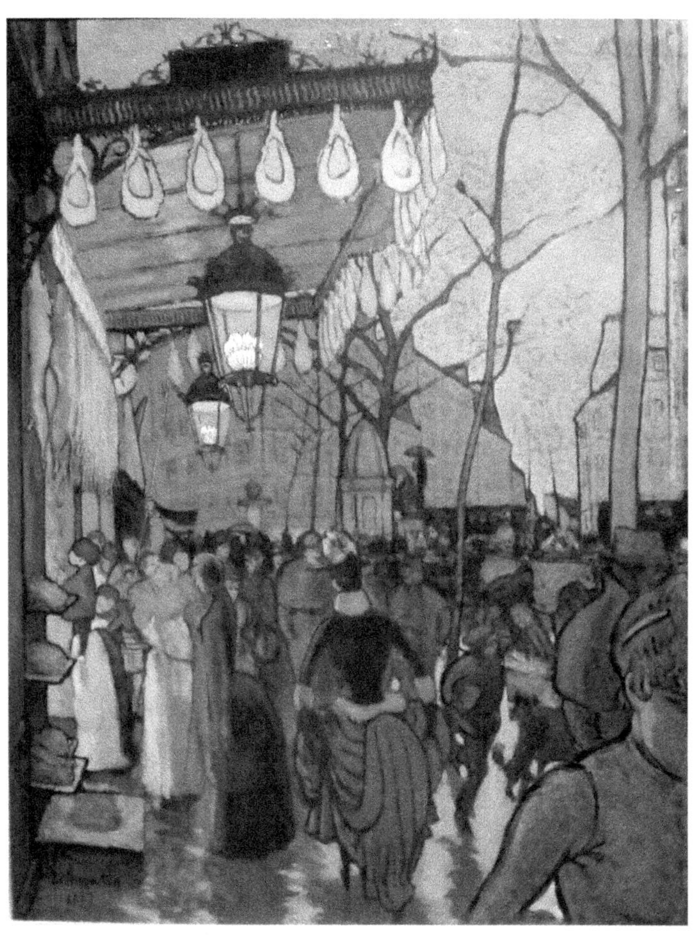

PAINTING: Avenue de Clinchy is Anquetin’s most famous painting—perhaps because of Van Gogh’s 1888 painting of the same name which was patterned very closely to Anquetin’s.

Emile Bernard

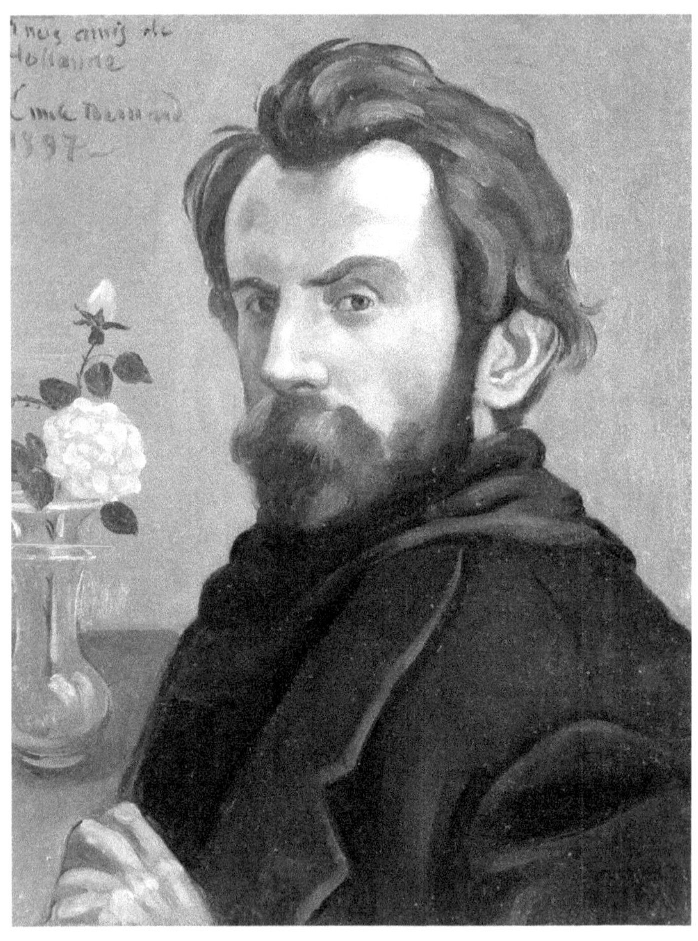

Self Portrait (1897)
Emile Bernard
Oil on canvas, "20.5 x 16.5"

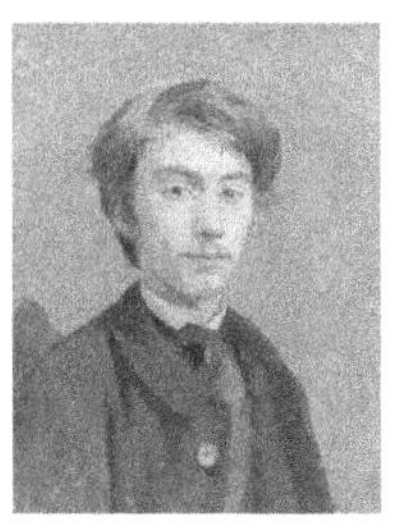

Emile Bernard

"Art has been the battle of my whole life."

Emile Bernard was nineteen when Les Petits Boulevards opened. He was from a moderately affluent bourgeois family who actively supported his art career. When he was only ten, they moved to Paris for him to assume serious art study.

Like the other painters of the exhibition, he studied with the Fernand Cormon Atelier group. He enrolled in Cormon after being expelled from the École des Beaux- Arts for showing "expressive tendencies" in his landscape paintings. Despite his age, he was probably the most intellectually gifted of the group, and along with Louis Anquetin was a founder of Synthetism, which was to evolve into 20th Century Expressionism.

Despite his young age, Bernard was an intimate of some of the greatest painters of the era. Toulouse-Lautrec was a painting partner and he was one of Van Gogh's few friends. He was likely the person who introduced Van Gogh to Paul Gauguin. In retrospect, it was not the most fortuitous introduction.

Lautrec's portrait of him shows a serious young man looking intently at his portraitist. He is thin with a long face and a bushy head of hair with long dark eyebrows. Despite the serious expression of the portrait, he was known to have had an impish personality and was the originator of practical jokes perpetrated on his friends. Although he avoided most of the vices that tormented Lautrec and Van Gogh, he could not avoid an inflated ego that would plague him for the rest of his life.

In the two summers before Les Petits, Bernard trekked to Pont-Aven a popular art colony near the Brittany coast where he first met Paul Gauguin. He might have been also joined by Anquetin, and the foundations of Synthetism took hold. After the Van Gogh show, the area became a popular destination for the Synthetists movement, and Pont-Aven School was applied to the style of paintings.

He returned to Paris in the fall of 1887 and both he and Anquetin renounced both Impressionism and the Pointillism of Georges Seurat and Paul Signac for a new style they called Synthetism, which was vastly different in style from either the Impressionists or the Pointillists. Instead of subtle shadings of color and tone, Synthetist paintings were characterized by broad flat patterns of pure color. The mental focus of the artist was shifted from capturing the nuances of light given off by the subject to the artist's own expression of the subject. In many ways, the style was a precursor of Expressionism that was to dominate art for next thirty years.

Symbolism was also a key element in the Synthetist work and especially Bernard's. Following the Les Petits exhibition, his work was dominated by religious symbology and he became an ardent student of Christian mysticism and would settle in Egypt for ten years.

The *Les Petits Boulevards* show was the opportunity for Bernard and his compatriot Anquetin to show off their new paintings. Bernard was one of the few painters that sold work at the show. He along with Anquetin would have shown their new Synthetist work. His most famous painting *Bathers with Red Cow* was likely included in the show. The painting is very reminiscent of Cezanne's series of bather paintings with an added symbolic element of the red cow. The painting would have also caught the attention of Gauguin.

Another significant work, Iron Bridges at Asniéres was also painted that year and no doubt was included in the show. The painting, which is in the collection of the New York Museum of Modern Art, shows two silhouetted figures strolling toward the iron bridge.

Two years later, Bernard would show work in a second Synthetist exhibition organized by Gauguin. The exhibition, which would be later known as the Volpini Exhibition, was held during the 1889 Exposition Universelle, the Paris World Fair. Bernard included 23 paintings in the exhibition, but apparently none sold.

After Volpini, the Les Petits artists went their separate ways, and in a dozen years, Van Gogh, Gauguin and Lautrec would all be dead.

The Synthetist style was to dominate his work for a few more years, but all of the attention was directed to Gauguin and later to the new Expressionists. Like his friend Anquetin, Bernard became disillusioned with the modernist movement and returned to more classical work. It is this abjuration of his own work that is largely responsible for the underappreciation of his artistic contributions to modern art.

An avid letter-writer, he would publish his correspondence with many of the leading modernists including Van Gogh, Gauguin, and Cezanne among others.

He devoted his final years to more intellectual pursuits and was a respected teacher for the next fifty years. For an artist who would live into his 80s, it is strange and somewhat sad that his greatest paintings were finished before he was twenty. The artist himself claimed before *Impressionists of the Petits Boulevards* that “my own talent was already fully developed.” One may speculate that this attitude did little to serve a career that had begun so brilliantly to ultimately fade into near oblivion.

Bathers with Red Cow (1887)
Emile Bernard, Oil on canvas, 36.3 × 28.8”

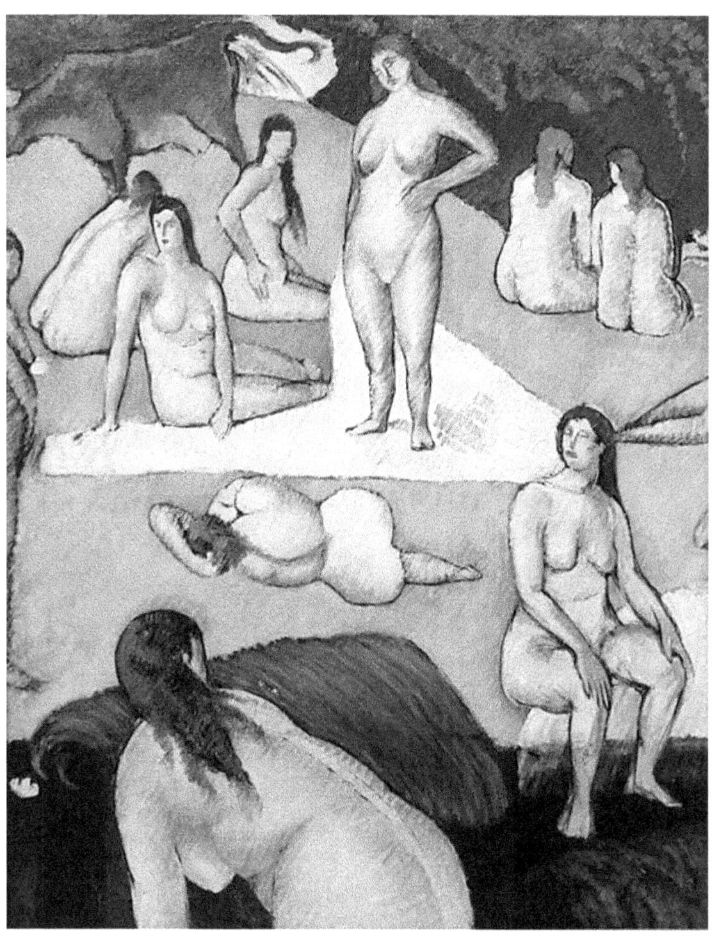

PAINTING: Bathers with Red Cow was Bernard’s homage to Cezanne, and is Bernard’s most famous painting.

Paul Gauguin

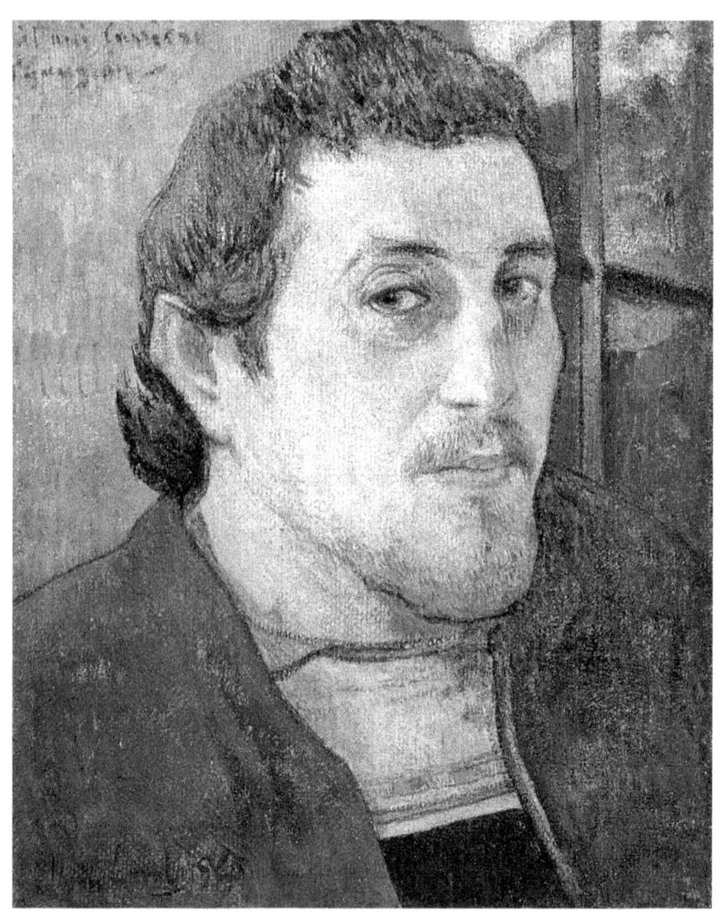

Self Portrait (1889)

Paul Gauguin

Oil on canvas, "20.5 x 16.5""

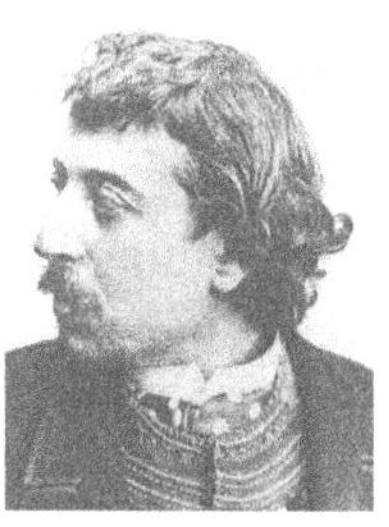

Paul Gauguin

"We never know what stupid is
until we have experimented on ourselves."

Paul Gauguin was thirty-nine when he returned to Paris just before the opening of *Les Petits Boulevards*. He had spent much of the year in Martinique where he had begun his quest of painting primitive cultures. While there, he completed a dozen or so paintings, but he was afflicted with dysentery and marsh fever. He returned to Paris with the hope of restoring his health and career.

Two years earlier, a business venture in Denmark had failed and Gauguin left his wife of eleven years and their five children. In the 1870s, he worked as an amateur artist, and he painted with the likes of Camille Pissarro and Paul Cezanne, and participated in several Parisian exhibitions. Like Van Gogh, Gauguin came to Paris to establish a career in art and like Van Gogh he had failed in most everything he had ever attempted, including several business ventures.

When he first returned to Paris, Gauguin resumed his friendship with Emile Bernard and Louis Anquetin, and no doubt would have attended the Les Petits exhibition. His friendship with Anquetin and Bernard would have a profound influence on Gauguin. Bernard later introduced him to his immediate circle of friends including Van Gogh, which would have a fateful impact on both of their lives. In his art, Gauguin would shortly receive validation for his new work which embraced the early principles of Cloisonnism, a style of painting with bold and flat forms and colors separated by dark contours. The style would evolve into a related movement called *Synthetism*, which added an emphasis on symbology and personal interpretation.

Synthetism was a predecessor to Twentieth Century Expressionism, and Gauguin has long been regarded as its most significant proponent. Much of this significance is probably related to his documented notoriety in French Polynesia where he carried on affairs with multiple pubescent girls whom he painted. It is this artistic imagery that gained Gauguin his widespread fame. Both Bernard and Anquetin believed that he arrogated the recognition that rightfully belonged to them. It was this ill feeling that led to both of them disavowing Synthetism for more classical styles.

Following the exhibition, Gauguin and Van Gogh would both leave Paris for Arles where they would live together for nine weeks. It was not a compatible match, and it was a time of constant tumult. The hostility came to a head when Van Gogh threatened Gauguin with a razor. This ultimately resulted with Van Gogh mutilating his ear and subsequent hospitalization. With Van Gogh hospitalized, Gauguin left Arles, never to see Van Gogh again. Gauguin would later recount his experiences in an apologetic book in which he claims to have exercised a heavy influence on Van Gogh's art.

Gauguin returned to Paris where he reconnected with Bernard and Anquetin and continued their exploration of Synthetism. In summers he would sojourn to Pont- Aven on the western French coast where he was treated like a hero by the young artists who flocked there. Pont-Aven became associated with Gauguin and Synthetism and the art is sometimes referred to as the School of Pont-Aven.

In the few years that Gauguin remained in France, he would paint The Yellow Christ, considered one of his most significant paintings. The painting depicts the crucifixion of Christ, and includes multiple characteristics for which he became famous. It is a symbolic piece that shows Christ on the cross surrounded by French peasant women in prayer. With its flat broad colors and dark outlines, it is a prototypical Synthetist painting. The Christ figure itself came from a Pont-Aven wood sculpture.

In the summer of 1889, Gauguin organized an exhibition called T*he Group of Impressionists and Synthetists*, later to be referred to as the Vulpine Exhibition. The exhibition was held during the Exposition Universelle, the Paris World Fair at the Cafe de Arts. The owner of the Cafe had originally planned to display a collection of ornate mirrors, but when they failed to arrive in time, Gauguin convinced the owner, Volpini, to provide the space for an art exhibition.

The exhibition was comprised of nine artists including Anquetin and Bernard, and his old friend Emile Schuffenecker. Gauguin showed 17 of his pieces. Like the *Les Petits*, the exhibition was a failure without a single sale. Despite the Volpini disappointment, Gauguin's reputation was on an upswing. While painting sales were still slow, they were promising. Nevertheless, he was growing impatient and his wanderlust struck him again. Claiming disappointment with the direction of European culture Gauguin, departed for Tahiti in 1891. He returned to France in 1893, where he painted several paintings depicting his observations and experiences in Tahiti. He returned to Tahiti in 1895, never to return to France.

In French Polynesia, he was continually in trouble with the local authorities, which eventually led to his arrest and conviction on a libel charge. In 1903, just before he was scheduled to begin his sentence, he died from a heart attack in addition to a plethora of other ailments.

The Yellow Christ (1889)
Paul Gauguin, Oil on canvas, 35.9 × 28.9”

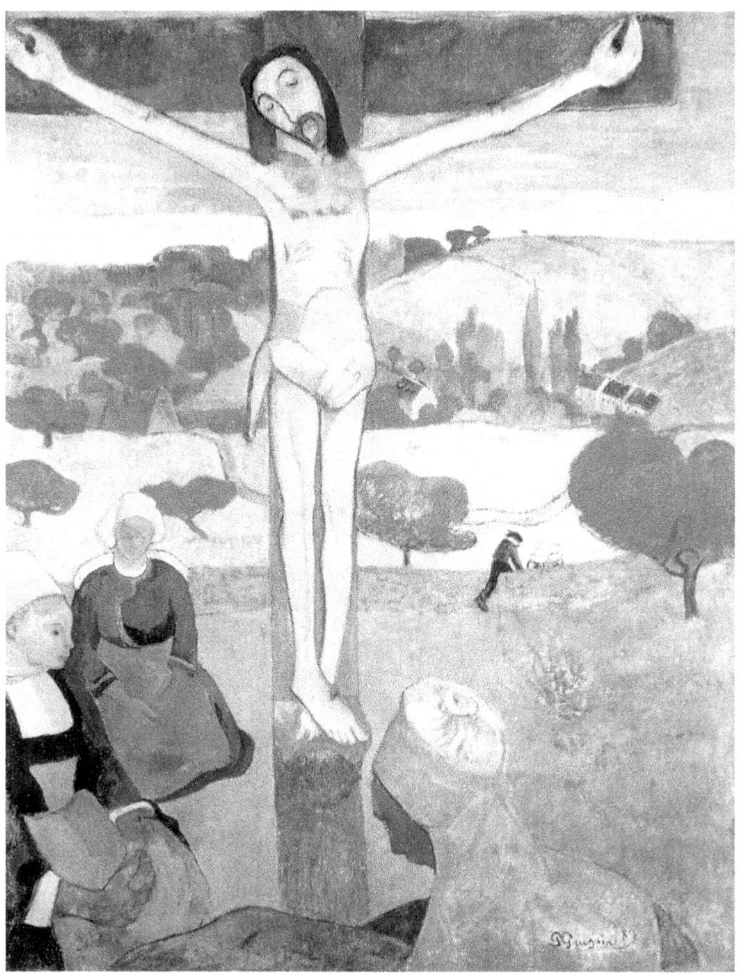

PAINTING: Yellow Christ has been cited as a quintessential Cloisonnist work, Gauguin reduced the image to areas of single colors separated by heavy black.

Suzanne Valadon

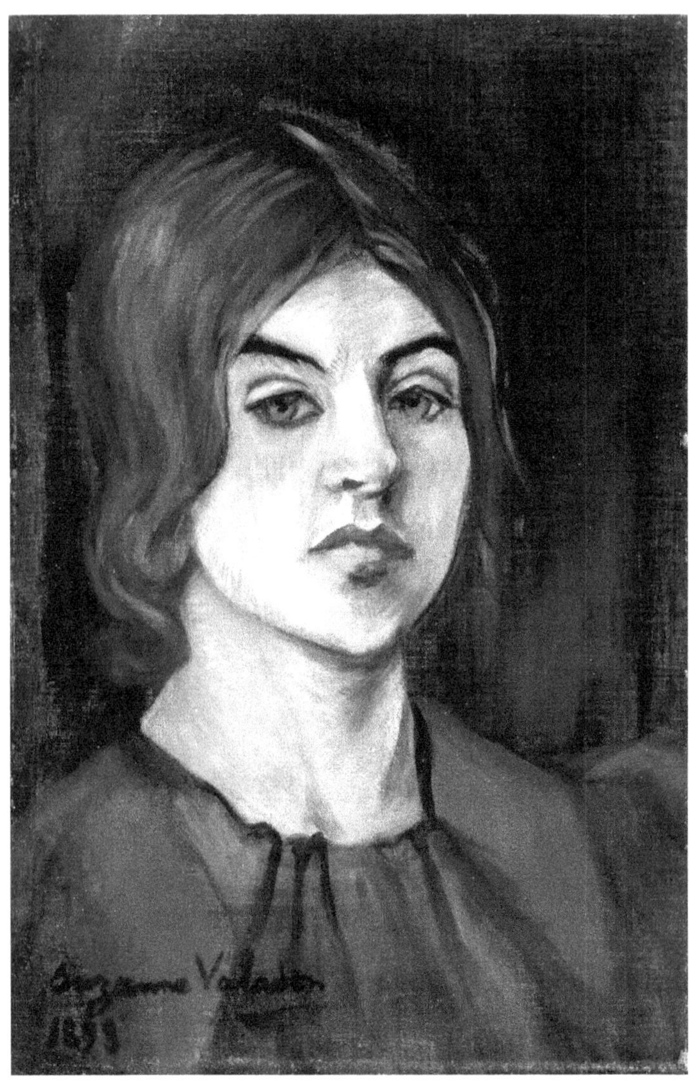

Self Portrait

Suzanne Valadon

Oil on canvas, "15.75 x 10..5"

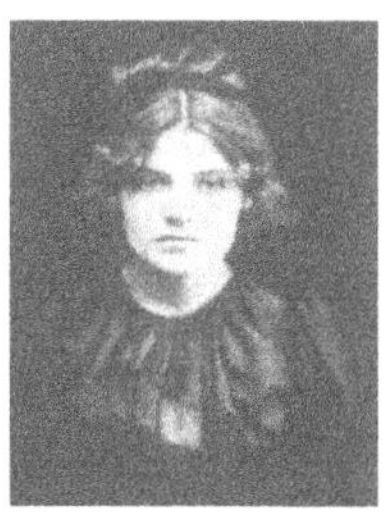

Suzanne Valadon

"I had great masters, I took the best of them, of their teachings, of their examples, I found myself, I made myself, and I said what I had to say."

When the Les Petits exhibition opened, Suzanne Valadon was one of Paris's most sought-after models. She was always attracted to the limelight and turned to modeling after suffering a serious fall as a circus acrobat. She was born Marie- Clémentine Valadon, the daughter of an unwed laundry lady. It was at Lautrec's suggestion that she changed her name to Suzanne, but he would still call her "Marie."

Valadon began modeling as a young teenager and quickly became the favorite of many of Paris's most popular artists. Renoir painted her in some of his most famous works. Toulouse-Lautrec befriended her and gave her drawing lessons. She modeled for at least two of Lautrec's paintings in the Les Petits exhibition. A free spirit and only 23, she had multiple liaisons with the artists for whom she modeled, including Renoir and perhaps Lautrec.

Valadon was one of those rare women who like a chameleon could transfigure herself into whatever woman an Suzanne Valadon artist or lover desired. She was attractive but not classicallybeautiful. She had dark brown hair, which she would often part in the middle with hanging bangs. She had an almost perfectly ovate face with high cheekbones and dark wide penetrating eyes. She was voluptuous in mind and body which added to her demand as a sculpture model.

Never devoid of ego and charisma, she would have attended the Les Petits exhibit to see Lautrec's paintings of her. She may have been involved in a romantic relationship with Lautrec, but monogamy was never one of her finer traits. With encouragement from her mother, she pushed for Lautrec to marry her. The fact that she would even contemplate the possibility shows her hubris and naiveté. Whatever their relationship, it would soon end and Lautrec would never mention her name again. There is no evidence that she modeled for any of the other artists in the show.

Following her breakup with Lautrec, Valadon moved on to Edgar Degas, who reportedly has little appreciation of Lautrec's work and life. Valadon was the model for Degas's most beautiful and passionate paintings including his famous bather paintings. Throughout their lives, Valadon and Degas remained friends and he was the last painter for whom she would model.

Much has been made of Degas's misogyny but his friendships with Valadon and earlier with Mary Cassatt were as strong as any of his male friendships. Socially, Valadon and Cassatt were as far apart as any two women, and each would have had little use for the other. Yet, Degas detected a rebellious spirit in each which underpinned the friendships. He taught both artists, and was an early collector of Valadon's work, and encouraged others to support her as well.

With the support of Degas, Valadon began showing her own work in the 1890s, and started recruiting female models to pose nude for her. Although her closest ties were with Paris's Impressionist painters, she would choose a different artistic expression. The Synthetist paintings of Bernard and Anquetin must have made a strong impression, because her own work would ultimately show many of the characteristics of these painters.

In 1904, Valadon had her first gallery show which was arranged by Degas's dealer at his request. At that time, much had changed in the French art-scape. Van Gogh, Lautrec and Gauguin were dead. Bernard and Anquetin had disavowed Synthetism, while Expressionism had replaced Impressionism as the new "ism." Her work continued to show many elements of Synthetism along with the new Expressionism. Valadon developed her distinctive art style which included symbolic and surreal elements with psycho-sexual overtones.

A decade earlier, after a rocky eight-year courtship, she married Paul Mousis, a rich banker and something of an art groupie. The marriage allowed Valadon to continue to paint without the pressures of selling. A few months into her marriage, a new man came into Valadon's life. Erik Satie, an art school drop-out, was only 21 when he met Valadon. He became immediately infatuated with her and shortly was accepted in what became an open ménage à trios. Apparently, Mousis accepted the situation, but Satie tired of sharing Valadon and left the ménage.

A final love interest came in the person of Andre Utter, who was introduced to Valadon by her son Maurice. Utter was half her age and was to be her great love. In 1909, she quickly divorced Mousis, and in 1915 she married Utter. For the next three decades, she shared exhibits with him until their divorce in 1934. She died four years later at the age of 73. Her only child was Maurice Utrillo, who would establish his own important art career.

Art history books rarely mention Valadon as an important contributor and innovator in Expressionist painting. It is an omission that is unfair and unfortunate. She was the first major female artist to incorporate female nudes into her work. Because of this, she was often criticized for being "too masculine." Despite this criticism, she was admired by her male contemporaries and was the first woman to be accepted into the Société Nationale des Beaux-Arts.

Portrait of the Family (1912)
Suzanne Valadon, Oil on canvas, 35.9 × 28.9”

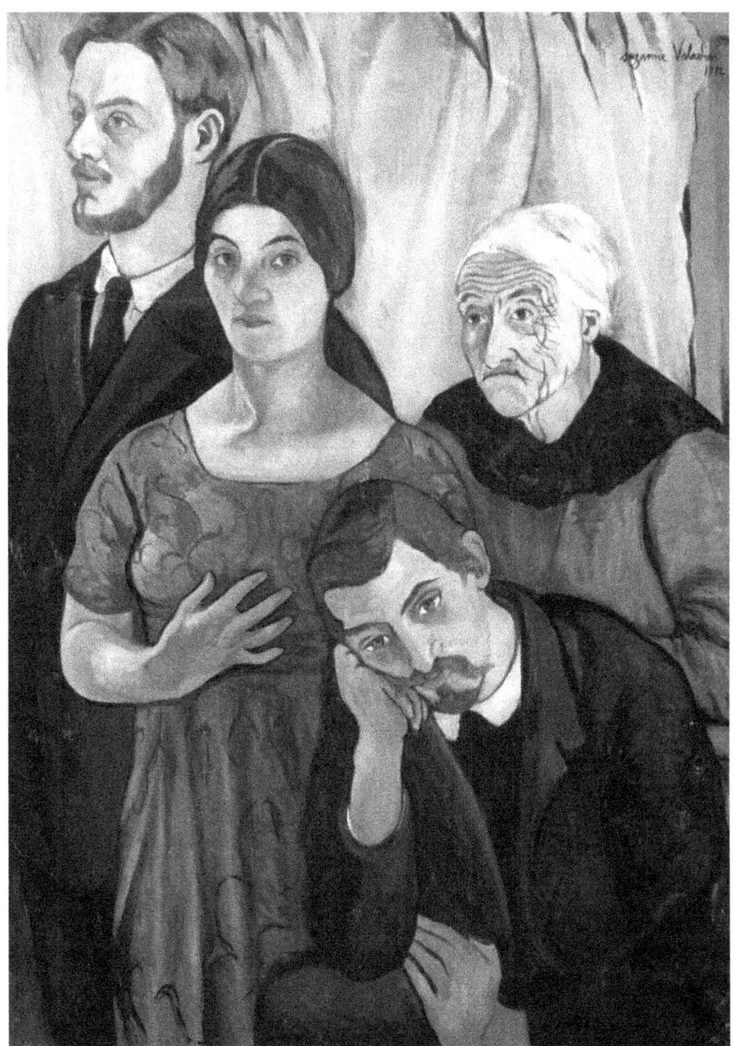

PAINTING: One happy family? Suzanne with Andre Utter (upper left), her mother and son Maurice Utrillo.

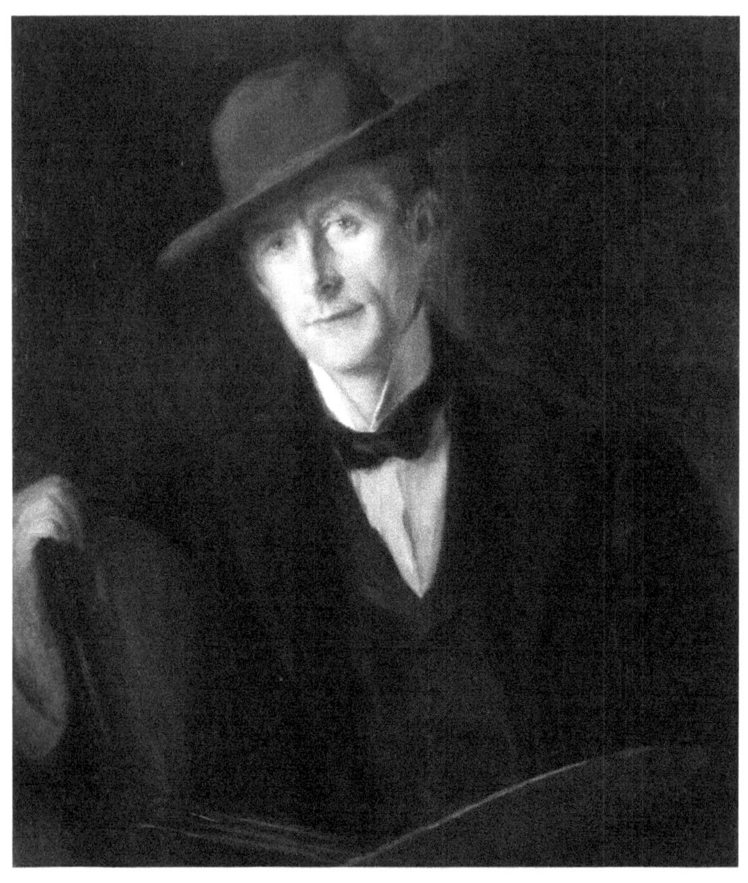

Walter Sickert
Jacque-Emile Blanche
Oil on canvas, "15.75 x 10..5"

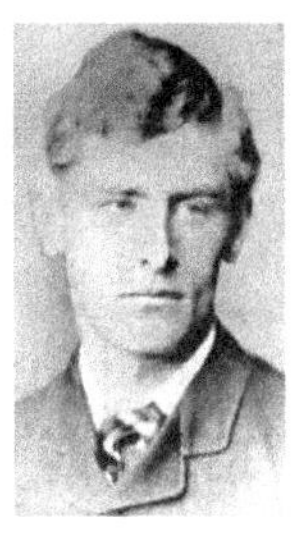

Walter Sickert

"All the great draughtsmen tell a story."

Born in Germany and raised in England, Walter Sickert was an aficionado of French culture and art. At the opening of Les Petits Boulevards, Sickert was twenty-seven and was just embarking on his art career. He came from a long line of artists, but as a young man aspired to be an actor, but after a brief association with a theater company and a few bit parts, he decided to pursue a career as a fine artist.

In his early twenties, he would assist James McNeill Whistler with his etchings. The relationship would evolve into a friendship and Whistler would serve as an important mentor. Whistler wrote letters of introduction that allowed Sickert to meet both Edouard Manet and Edgar Degas in Paris. Much of the 1880s were spent in France, where he was to meet many of the rising Impressionists.

Sickert would also join Whistler on his regular visits to see Elizabeth Forbes in Pont-Aven. Like Whistler, she worked as a printmaker and was a member of the Society of Painter Etchers in London. Besides her artistic talent,

Forbes was beautiful and possessed a charismatic personality which attracted a coterie of admireres. On these frequent sojours, It is likely that Sickert would have crossed paths with both Emile Bernard and Louis Anquetin, who were also frequent visitors of the seacoast city.

Sickert was a tall, handsome man who could have been a star in Hollywood if he had been born a century later. A photographic portrait in 1894 shows an attractive face with a strong jaw and nose, but with fine lips and penetrating deep-set eyes. No doubt, he had little trouble attracting women, and would marry three times.

Besides his association with Whistler, Sickert was most influenced by Degas, whose pastel tonality was consonant with Sickert's dark, moody oils. While many of Impressionists, such as Monet, avoided narrative, Sickert thought it was the soul of art and he claimed his work and all significant art should present the human condition in a way that words could not. "All the great draughtsmen tell a story." Like Degas, his paintings presented an ambiguous narrative, and at times a misogynistic narrative

Sickert no doubt knew all of the French artists in the Les Petits exhibition, and he would later develop a friendship with Lautrec. However, it is doubtful that the work, especially Bernard's and Anquetin's, would have elicited a positive reaction since he was grounded on a more tonal Impressionism as opposed to the pure colors of Synthetism. Nor was Sickert a great fan of Van Gogh's work, especially of the artist's impasto (thick application of paint). He described his reaction to the paintings of Van Gogh: "I execrate his treatment of the instrument I love. These strips of metallic paint that catch the light like so many dyed straws sets my teeth on edge"

For Van Gogh color was everything; for Sickert it was nothing. Hardly a breath of color reaches his canvas, and a survey of his work shows almost a total exclusion of landscape or any natural setting. Even when he visited Venice, he quickly became bored with the canals, and instead painted prostitutes in seedy brothels.

His personality matched his paintings. He had a dark brooding personality and was quick to find fault in artwork outside of the gloomy tonal work of the Impressionism of Degas and Whistler.

After *Les Petits*, Sickert would return to England and assume a life as a professional painter. He would join the New English Art Club, whose art was heavily influenced by the French realist painters such as Degas and even Lautrec. Like Lautrec, the stage served as a fertile source of many of his first works, which included Katie Lawrence at the Gatti's. The painting, depicting a popular stage performer, was panned by the critics as being "vulgar, tawdry and ugly."

He was a founding member of the Camden Town Group of painters. The group was named after a section of London where many of the artists lived. The area was also famous as the scene of the Jack the Ripper murders and the less publicized Whitechapel murders. Sickert's paintings of abject apartment interiors and women in distress have been associated Sickert with these crimes, and he has been accused as the perpetrator.

As he aged, he became even more staid in his personality and attitudes. He was a conservative art critic and had little use for the new post-Impressionist and modern painters. He was particularly critical of Henri,Matisse and]Picasso, and the modern movement in general. Despite marital and financial difficulties, he continued to paint and teach until he died in 1942 at the age of 81. Appreciation for his work was primarily restricted to England where his reputation was based as much on his printmaking as for his painting. Today, his fame or infamy is clouded by the whole Jack the Ripper controversy.

The Studio: The Painting of the Nude (1906)
Walter Sickert, Oil on canvas, 31.87 × 25.5”

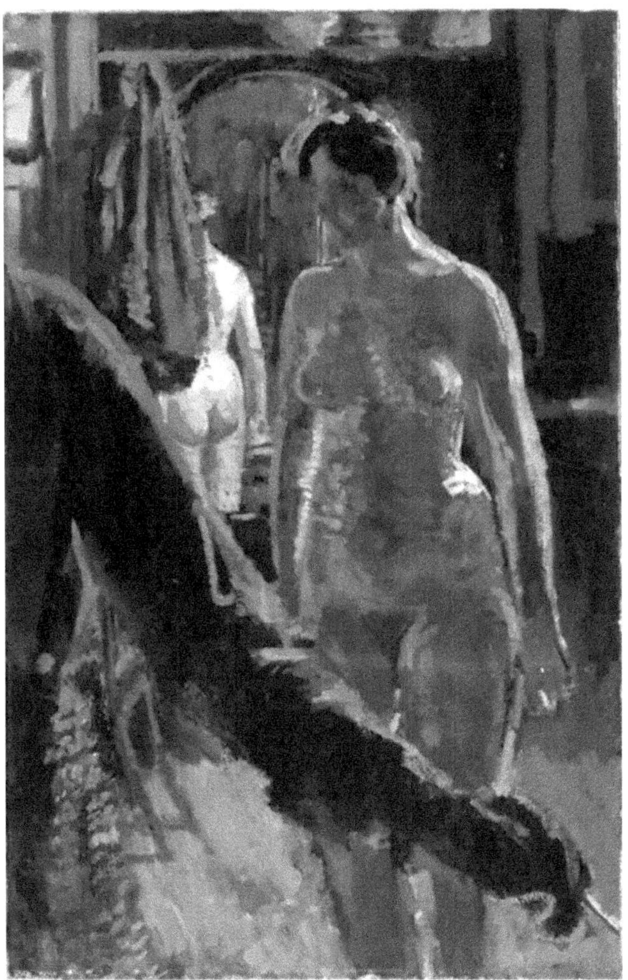

PAINTING: Sickert’s portrayal of women always have acourse, carnal edge. In Painting the Nude, the posture and presentation of his model is typical of that portrayal.

Misia Godebska (Natanson, Sert)

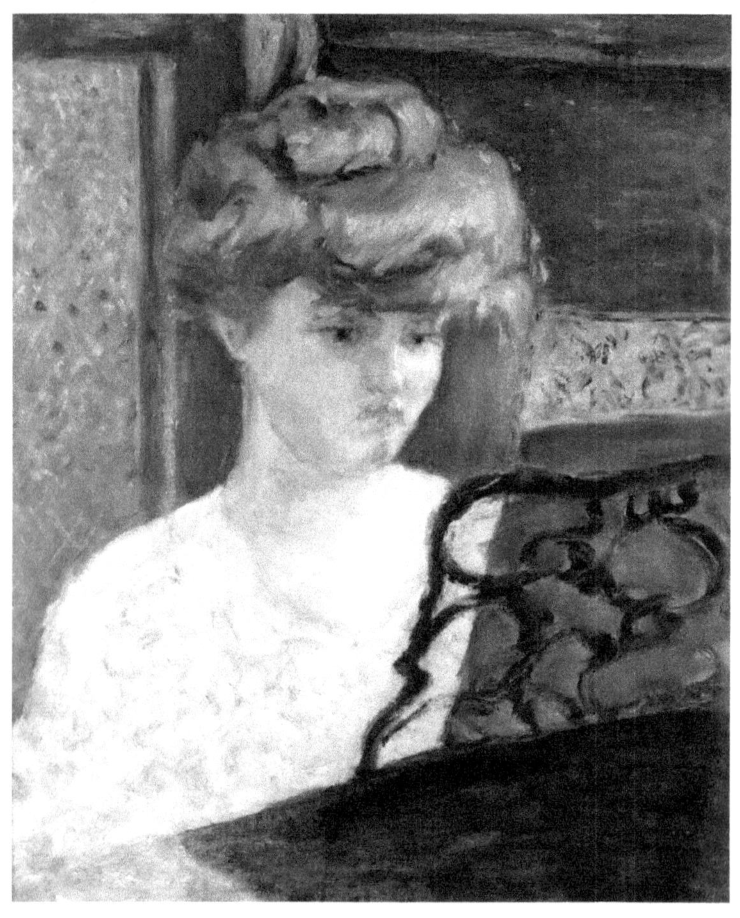

Misia at the Piano
Jacque-Pierre Bonnard
Oil on canvas, "15.75 x 10..5"

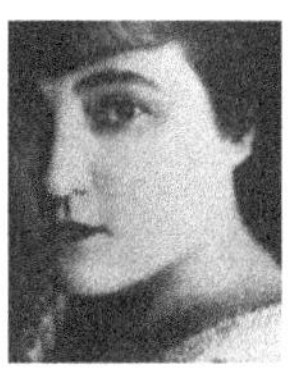

Misia Godebska

"I don't respect art, I love it."

Misia Godebska was only fifteen when *Les Petits* opened. She was the daughter of Polish sculptor Cyprien Godebski and Zofia Servais. Misia inherited her musical talent from her mother's family where her grandfather was the noted Belgian cellist Adrien-François Servais.

Her mother died at childbirth and Misia was shipped off to live with her grandparents in Belgium. These early years with her grandparents were dominated by a life of music. Misia was something of a prodigy, and she would often perform for the noted musicians who visited the household. In her later years, she would recount how she sat on the lap of the great pianist Franz Liszt and played Beethoven.

For the first decade of her life, she was ignored by her father who married several times and had dozens of liaisons. When she was nine he reclaimed her and brought her to Paris. Perhaps, if she would have been allowed to remain in Brussels, she would have gone on to become one of the great pianists of the 20th Century.

In Paris, she was placed in a convent boarding school

where her only escape was her weekly piano lessons with Gabriel Fauré whose interest was probably based as much on her beauty as her talent. When she was 15, she fled to London with money she borrowed from friends, but later in the year returned to Paris where she emancipated herself from her father. To support herself, she taught students whom Fauré referred.

She was tall for her age with a voluptuous figure that still retained a hint of prepubescence. She wore her thick auburn hair in a high bun, which accentuated her neck and shoulders—her best features. Her face was full and round with a pert nose and a bit of a short chin—not a classical beauty but already with a sultriness that would attract the greatest artists of her age.

The *Les Petits* exhibition could have inaugurated her entrance into the world of the flourishing art community of Paris. Her fame will be achieved through her beauty and charisma, and although she would play the piano for her friends and guests, she would never appear on the concert stage. Where she did appear on the canvases of many of the aspiring Impressionist painters of the day. Renoir, Bonnard, Lautrec, Vuillard all painted her portrait on multiple occasions. Even Picasso fell under her charms and would devote a canvas to her and she was the godmother to his first son.

Not only did these artists seek to paint her but also to seduce her. Although sexual adventures would appear later, in these early years she resisted these advances. Even the great womanizer, Picasso, could only be a friend. Of all ofher admirers, the most ardent was Edouard Vuillard who devoted endless canvases to her as well as hundreds of photographs capturing the coterie that evolved around her. On her first marriage to Thaddie Natanson, he broke down and wept inconsolably.

Misia was never a professional model and agreed to pose for the friendship and the fame that it afforded. The portraits were all formal and no doubt staged by her. Renoir pleaded to paint her nude, but to his regret and the others, she would never succumb to their pleas.

Using the wealth of a series of rich husbands, she would become the center of Paris's artistic society. To be invited to one of her regular salons was viewed as a great honor that no artist would refuse. With her first husband Thaddie Natanson, they established the La Revue Blanche magazine whose contributors included many of Paris's most celebrated artists. Lautrec's portrait of Misia graced one of its covers.

When Thaddie encountered financial problems, he was rescued by the newspaper magnate, Alfred Edwards, who provided the money on the condition that he give up his claim to Misia. After the divorce, she married Edwards in 1905, and she became the matriarch of Paris's cultural society. Maurice Ravel dedicated *Le Cygne* (The Swan) and *La Valse* (The Waltz). Misia continued to grace the cover of *La Revue Blanch*. At one of her salons, she accompanied Enrico Caruso on the piano while the opera star entertained her guests with a repertory of Neapolitan songs.

Her marriage to Edwards didn't last five years as Edwards proved to be a faithless husband. They divorced in

1909. She would marry one more time in 1920 to José María Sert, a Spanish society artist. Although the marriage lasted only a few years, they remained friends for the rest of their lives. For the next 30 years, Misia Sert dominated the arts scene of Paris. She survived the Nazi occupation of Paris with her reputation intact while many in her circle were accused of collaboration. She died in 1950 at the age of seventy-eight in Paris. Her long-time friend and occasional lover, Coco Chanel dressed Sert in her burial gown as Paris's artistic elite mourned her passing.

Misia Natanson (1897)
Henri Toulouse-Lautrec, Oil on canvas (Detail)

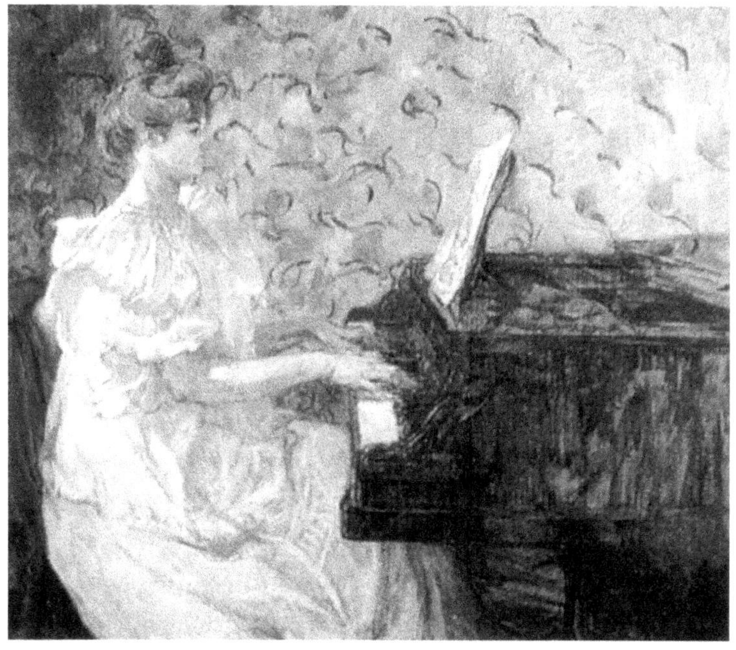

PAINTING: Lautrec was known to paint unflattering portraits of the women in his life. His obvious affection for Misia shows in Misia Natanson, which he painted ten years after Les Petits.

James Whistler

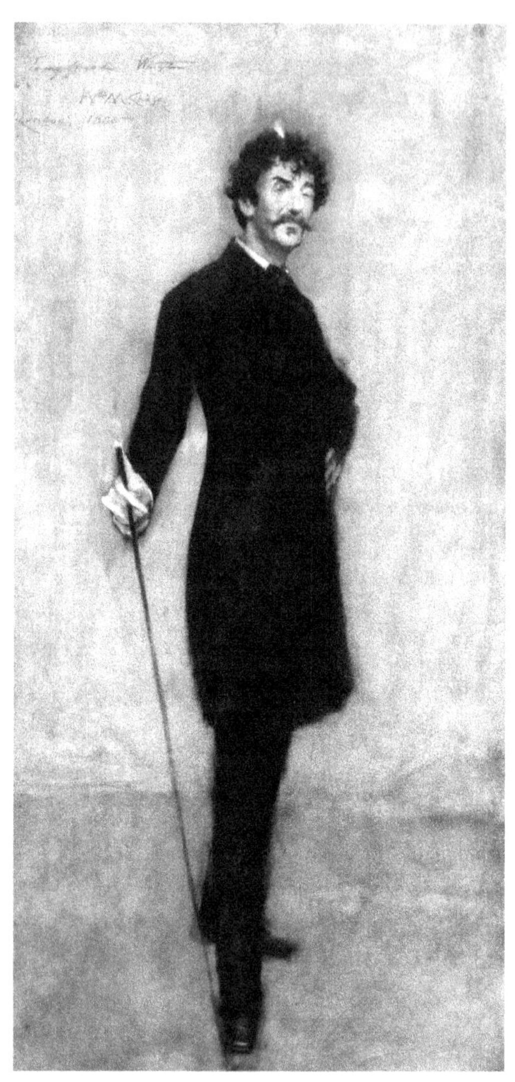

James Abbott McNeil Whistler
William Merritt Chase
Oil on canvas, "74.75 x 36.25"

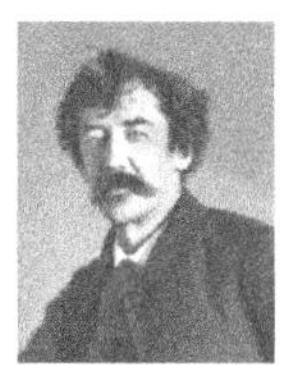

James Whistler

"I can't tell you that genius is hereditary because heaven has granted me no offspring."

American James Abbott McNeill Whistler came to Paris to paint in 1855, and never returned to America. He is most remembered for his work and exploits in England, but much of his European life was spent in France and particularly in Paris. At the time of the Les Petits, he was fifty-three and very well known and appreciated by the French art community. He was very good friends with Degas and many of the other important French Impressionists. Lautrec would become a friend and visit Whistler in his home in England. It was Whistler who sent several letters of introduction for his friend and protégé Walter Sickert when Sickert visited Paris.

Although he is most famous for his portraits, (his painting of his mother is one of the most famous art images ever produced), he was also an important etcher and lithographer. He even experimented with photography and used it as a tool in his painting, but never in portrait work which was always done live. It was said there was nothing more excruciating than sitting for a Whistler portrait, because of the abuse the sitter would frequently receive from him.

He was also a great nocturne painter with the work receiving much praise and much criticism. Whistler himself coined the name “nocturne,” for any painting of night or twilight. He used the term when the painting conveyed a dreamy, pensive mood. He would also include musical expressions such as "symphony" in the title.

Like his contemporary Oscar Wilde, he was almost ruined by a frivolous lawsuit. In 1877, art critic John Ruskin made some disparaging comments about a Whistler nocturne painting that was exhibited in a recent gallery show. Ruskin criticism, published in Fors Clavigera, a London arts newspaper, questioned the value of the art. Ruskin concluded, “I have seen, and heard, much of Cockney impudence before now; but never expected to hear a coxcomb ask two hundred guineas for flinging a pot of paint in the public’s face.” Whistler sued Ruskin for libel and hoped to receive 1000 pounds and legal costs. After a long extended trial, Whistler was awarded a farthing (less than a penny) and legal costs were split. Whistler recounted the trial in his book, *The Gentle Art of Making Enemies*. Making enemies was a skill very well honed by Whistler.

The trial and its verdict devastated Whistler financially and he was depressed and distraught for several months. However, a commission for twelve Venice pieces rescued him. He and his paramour Maude Franklin found rooms in a dilapidated palazzo they shared with other artists, among them was John Singer Sargent. Getting out of London for a time was probably the best cure for his financial and artistic constitution. He stayed over a year, and it was the most productive period of his life. Whistler finished fifty etchings, and over 100 paintings, most of them pastels, but also a few oils and watercolors.

In 1885, he wrote his first book, *Ten O'clock Lecture*. Wilde gave the book a laudatory review, and perhaps too laudatory, and Whistler thought he was being mocked. The incident caused the collapse of their friendship, and they scrabbled at each other for the remainder of their days. Wilde perhaps got the best insult when he used Whistler as the arrogant artist in his most famous novel, *The Portrait of Dorian Grey.*

A self-professed dandy, he held forth in Paris as much as in London, and to be included in a Whistler soirée was considered a real honor for the recipient. Besides his obvious talents as a painter, he had a sharp wit that would outdo the likes of Oscar Wilde who also made Paris a second home. He was welcomed in the homes of nobility as well as those in the arts and politics. Although over 50, he enjoyed the company of young women and he was in the process of breaking up with his mistress Maude Franklin, who had been his companion for nearly a decade.

Whistler became increasingly interested in using photography as a tool, and he appreciated the atmospheric quality, especially for his night scenes. Although most of his nocturnes were painted from English scenes, it was very possible that he could have gone to Paris to research night scenes for a new series. A year after *Les Petits*, he dumped

Maud Franklin who had been his constant companion for the past ten years, and the mother of his two daughters. Franklin never quite fit in with Whistler's society, and her years with him aged her.

Shortly thereafter, Whistler married Beatrix Goodwin, a prominent socialite and the widow of his architect friend E.W. Goodwin. It was his only marriage, and by all accounts a happy one. With her social connections, Whistler's financial situation improved. In 1890, he wrote the satiric book, *The Gentle Art of Making Enemies*. He had much greater success in making enemies than the book did in making profits, but it did generate modest sales. Five years into his marriage to Goodwin, she developed cancer, and her death proved devastating to him personally and for his art.

In the last decade of his life, he did little serious painting, except for a few small seascape watercolors. He experimented with color photography, concentrating on his favorite subjects, beautiful women and London architecture. After a long period of ill health, he died in 1903 at the age of sixty-nine.

Arrangement in White and Black (1876)
James Whistler, Oil on canvas, 75.5 × 36”

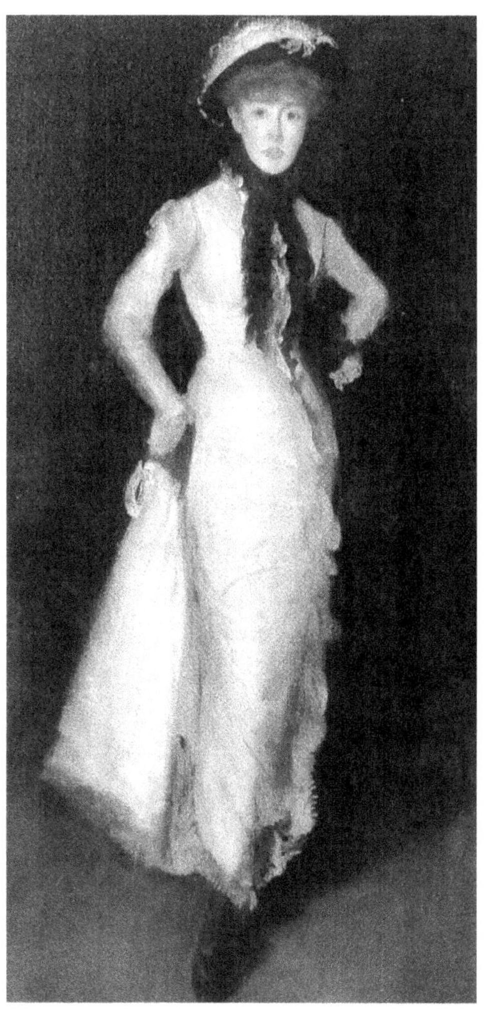

PAINTING: Whistler met Maude Franklin in the early 1870's when she was fifteen. She was the model for one of his most famous paintings, "Arrangement in White and Black."

Novella

Vam Gogh's Show
Impressionists of the Petits Boulevards

Morning
Afternoon
Evening

Morning

Vincent Van Gogh awoke in a bad mood. He went to bed without adding wood to the small stove that heated his sparse flat which also served as his studio. He shivered most of the night in the cold, and hardly slept more than a few hours, despite the copious amounts of cognac he consumed at Du Chalet.

He and his brother Theo hung the exhibition the night before, and the two argued all evening. At midnight the tension came to a head with a final blowup and Theo stormed out, forcing Vincent to hang the rest of the show by himself. Hanging the show by candlelight was difficult, and he was now having second thoughts about the placement of some of his pieces.

Even when he did sleep, he was plagued with unsettling dreams. All of these dreams had a constant theme —collectors deriding his work. In some of the dreams, there was silent mocking, but in the last dream there was outright laughter which awoke him.

He staggered to the wash basin across the room. He poured water into the basin and splashed it on his face. It was frigid and shocked him out of his slumber. He looked athis reflection in the broken mirror above the basin. He was surprised to see an old man peering back at him. Not even forty, he looked twenty years older. His eyes were heavily bloodshot and his skin was ashen, almost like a corpse. His teeth hurt and felt loose as he tested them with the base of his thumb.

He glanced at the wall clock and was disappointed to see that it was only eight o'clock. The show would officially open at two o'clock in the afternoon, and then afterwards the artists were going to Lautrec's studio for a post-opening party. He hated these get-togethers where everyone talked about art. He was more interested in showing it, especially his own which he always brought in rolled canvases. His French was barely passable, and he always felt out of place with these artists who were much younger and more sociable. Most evenings, he would leave abruptly with his unseen canvases curled under his arms.

He was still bothered by his dreams and he was anxious about the reception for the show and his pieces in particular. Perhaps, he included too many figurative works and should have shown more Parisian cityscapes—collectors seem to be gravitating toward them. He wanted very much to sell some work instead of having to rely on his brother for support.

Thoughts of Theo evoked memories of their time last night. How could he hate a brother he loved so much? The prospect of seeing Theo at the show upset him, but who else would sell his work?

On his easel stood a blank canvas. He always felt better when he painted and scanned the flat to find something topaint. A withered bunch of sunflowers were lying on the table and he thought they could make a good painting on this cold and gray November morning. His spirits improved with the thought of doing some painting. He felt a slight pang of hunger, but he would have a bowl of soup at the restaurant before the show opened.

His mind returned to the large ballroom that served as the gallery for the exhibition. He closed his eyes and imagined a room full of enthusiastic collectors surrounding his work.

"I think they will like my pictures. Perhaps even sell a piece or two," he thought as he gathered wood for his oven.

Henri Toulouse-Lautrec sat at the small desk reading a letter by the light of the only window in his studio. It was from his mother in Malromè. In the letter, she hopes that he will have a fine birthday, but she warns of the dangers of over-celebration. He passes quickly over this paragraph, and he rereads, “Your father will probably attend the opening of your Paris show.”

Lautrec mused out loud, “Probably attend.” There was never anything definite about his father. Although he had received a letter from him every few weeks, he had not seen his father in six months. The prospect of having his father at his first major exhibit excited him, but he also found the prospect disturbing.

He had often attributed much of his artistic talent from his paternal lineage, but his father had only tepidly supported his decision to become an artist. Of course, his father never fully supported him in anything.

He had resisted the temptation to go out drinking the night before despite it being his twenty-third birthday. Although he had real issues with his family, he would have enjoyed the attention they would have lavished on him. Louis Anquetin had offered to take him out to dinner, but Lautrec declined. Instead, after the opening this afternoon, his friends would return to his studio to celebrate his birthday and hopefully the success of their show.

He thought of the paintings that Van Gogh had selected for the show. They were all figurative pieces with two paintings of Suzanne Valadon. The images of both of these paintings floated to his mind. He was pleased with the works, but would they sell? Probably not—but he did not care.

"If no one else likes them, I know that Suzanne will," he muttered to himself. His mind drifted to Valadon who he had painted almost exclusively for the past few months. Although he paid her well, the relationship was more than an artist-model one. He liked her, but he did not love her. He certainly was attracted to her and would have liked to sleep with her but so would half of the artists in Montmartre. She had slept with Renoir, so why not him?

The other portrait in the show was one of his mother. He laughed, "My mother and my whore." He was pleased with the portrait, but he doubted his mother would. He thought his mother was an attractive woman, but the portrait was harsh without any tenderness. For a moment, he regretted making the piece so dour. He imagined her reaction if she saw the piece, and he was glad she would not attend the show. "But I am certain that she will send one of her spies to report back to her," he said aloud.

He checked the clock on the wall. It was only ten o'clock—four more hours until he needed to be at the exhibit. He was hungry, but he was drawn to a half-finished canvas on the easel.

Louis Anquetin hated being alone. Even when he painted, he was most comfortable when another artist was painting with him. It was only ten o'clock, and it would be another two hours before he would leave to meet Emile Bernard for lunch. He had already dressed for the engagement, and he strolled over to the full-length mirror to check out his outfit. He was pleased with his clothes, but wasn't certain whether he wanted to wear the top hat that sat on the table. He surveyed himself carefully with and without the hat. He was unable to make up his mind, and decided to let the weather determine his decision.

Unlike most of his artist friends, he was overly self-conscious of his dress. He even deliberated what to wear when he painted. He thought of himself as an actor who was on an ever-present stage before a critical audience whom he didn't want to disappoint. As he grew older, this egocentricity dominated his life. As long as he could remember, he was always the most handsome, the most talented and most appealing of human beings. It was an impression that he wished to retain.

Art was just one facet of this persona—albeit an important one. He was aware of his reputation as one of Paris's young ascending Impressionists. He also wanted to be recognized as one of its leading avant-garde artists, and Impressionism was becoming passé. His paintings in Van Gogh's show were a rejection of Impressionism, and he was uncomfortable with the risk that would be involved in showing the work. He did not handle rejection well, so he tried to push the thought from his mind.

He sat down on a large easy chair next to the studio's small bay window and lit a cigar. He looked outside and saw a gray sky and the day looked cold. He decided to wear the top hat. As he puffed the cigar, he reviewed in his mind his paintings in the show. Although he wasn't certain how this new style would be received, he was pleased with the work in this new style. He also tried to imagine the pieces that Bernard selected for the show. Obviously, this would be the work by which his would be judged. Of the four Bernard pieces, the only piece that concerned him was the large Red Cow canvas. Much of his work was smaller and would be dominated if placed next to Red Cow. Van Gogh and his brother had already hung the show, and there was a good possibility that they would have hung his and Bernard's pieces together. This thought bothered him, but it was too late to worry about that now.

Anquetin glanced back at the clock. Only a few minutes had passed since the last time he looked.

"Will this morning ever end," he murmured to himself.

Emile Bernard awoke just before sunrise. His sleep was troubled with thoughts of compositional problems with the painting on his easel. In his sleep, the solution had come to him in a flash, and he wanted to fix the piece before the solution disappeared. It was very simple. The painting depicted a young girl in a kimono reading a book. On the table next to her was a vase with a single stem of a bulbed flower that jutted straight up. What the piece needed was a second stem to tie all the elements together. It took only a few minutes to add the second stem. The house was quiet. He enjoyed these early morning times when he alone was awake. His grandmother tried to allow him as much personal space as possible, but when the rest of the household was active, it was sometimes difficult to concentrate on his painting and his thoughts. These early morning hours were usually devoted to thinking when tranquility was essential. When painting, he would fall into a creative trance that left him unaware of his surroundings.

He had already dressed in his finest black cashmere jacket with a dark maroon tie. He chose the outfit because he felt it added gravity to his appearance. Not even twenty, he was self-conscious of his age, especially when socializing with his friends who were usually much older. He looked into the full-length mirror that hung in the back of his studio. He detected a bit of stubble on his chin and he imagined how he would look with a beard or maybe a goatee. He sighed audibly and returned to the painting on the easel.

He was now pleased with the piece, and regretted that he had not completed it soon enough to include it in the show. Most of his pieces were his new Synthetist work, but his only figurative painting was a small impressionist piece of a young woman he completed a few years ago. For a moment he had an urge to put a frame on a new piece, and see if Van Gogh would exchange it for the Impressionist piece. He reconsidered the idea, and thought the old piece would serve to set off his new work.

He would not paint today. He and Anquetin had agreed to have lunch at the Restaurant du Chalet before viewing the show in the upstairs ballroom. A British friend of Anquetin's may also meet them for lunch. He could not remember whether Anquetin had ever mentioned his name, but it was a friend or associate of James Whistler.

He thought of the previous evening when he dropped off his paintings for the show. Van Gogh and his brother Theo had just begun to hang the paintings. The show had no official title, but Vincent had called it: The *Impressionists of the Petits Boulevards*. The title amused him. Indeed this was a petit show, but it was a stretch to call any of the artists, "Impressionists." He certainly did not think of himself as an impressionist, and the only true impressionist in the show was its only amateur, Arnold Koening. Although Bernard had exhibited in several student shows, this was his first "serious show." He thought for a moment whether the show would find its way into art history. He laughed at his own arrogance.

At that moment, his grandmother entered the room

Paul Gauguin awoke. There was no clock on the wall so he was not certain of the time. It was the second night in a row that he slept the full night without fever or chills. In the other room, he could hear the cheerful voices of the Schuffenecker children. Although the curtains were open, the room was dim and chilly. He quickly put on a thick wool robe that was draped over a chair next to the bed.

He walked over to the wash basin and splashed some water on his face. The water was ice-cold and it jolted him from his drowsiness. Above the basin was a small mirror. He looked at his reflection intently. Although his face was thin, almost emaciated, there was some semblance of color —not the ashen ghost that had greeted him for the past two weeks. He felt he was gaining some strength after his bout with dysentery.

He had a long face with sharpened features. His emaciation accentuated the sharpness, but even now he thought himself handsome. His dark brown eyes were wide-set, with arching long eyebrows and a bushy black mane. His mustache needed trimming and thick stubble covered his face. He decided it was time to shave.

Since arriving back in Paris from Martinique, he had stayed with Emile Schuffenecker and his family. Most of the time was spent in their small guest room where he was racked with fever and chills. Gratitude was not easy for him to express, but he was grateful for the kindness the family had shown him. He met Emile almost twenty years ago when they both worked at the same stock brokerage house. Although they had been successful brokers, both yearned to be artists.

Gauguin walked into the kitchen unnoticed. Louise Schuffenecker was washing the dishes and her two children were playing in the adjoining room. Their voices reminded him of his own children, and he was swept with a momentary longing to see them. But that longing and guilt quickly vanished. He turned his attention upon the woman, looking at him

"Good morning," she said with a pleasant smile.

She was an attractive woman with long auburn hair. She was tall and carried herself with grace. Gauguin often wondered how Emile had ever succeeded in marrying such a beautiful woman. Could he have abandoned her as he did his wife and children?

"Good morning," he replied. "How are you feeling?" She asked, handing him a cup of coffee she had just poured.

"Much better," he said as he sipped the coffee. "And thanks for this."

"You are welcome. You look much better. Emile and I were worried that we would have to take you to the hospital," she said, joining Gauguin at the kitchen table.

"I want to thank you for your gracious hospitality. I am not certain what I would have done if you would not have taken me in," he said, reaching over to touch her hands. They lingered for a few quiet moments.

"You know you are always welcome here," she replied looking squarely into his eyes.

"Do you have any plans today?"

"I think a long bath and a shave should be the first order

of business," he laughed. "And perhaps, this afternoon I'll join Louis Anquetin at an exhibition of his and a few of his artist friends."

"Are you certain that you are up to it?" She asked with concern in her voice.

"I feel much better, but I will see how I feel this afternoon— but now for my bath and shave."

"I will put on some hot water," she said. "I can shave you if you like."

"That would be very nice, but I think I can manage," he answered after a long pause.

Suzanne Valadon gazed at her mother on the other side of the kitchen table. It was not even ten o'clock and she had already begun to drink. "So why would this day be any different," she thought as she viewed her mother in disgust. She averted her eyes from the pitiable figure and caught a glimpse of herself in the broken mirror over the wash basin. It disturbed her to see how much she resembled her mother, whom she remembered as a beauty when they first arrived in Paris.

Although drinking and a difficult life had begun to harden her features, her mother was still an attractive woman. Suzanne inherited her mother's thick black hair and ovate face with full arching eyebrows. She also shared her mother's delicate lips and sensual mouth, but they rarely smiled, especially when they were together. Both were curvaceous with ample bosoms while Suzanne displayed the petite figure her mother once had.

She certainly had the money to leave her mother with the growing income she received as one of Paris's most popular models. But her mother was a convenient watcher for her young son, Maurice, when she modeled or partied in Montmartre.

"You will have to watch Maurice this afternoon. I will be at Restaurant du Chalet to see a new show with Lautrec with some of his Cormon friends," she informed her mother, who didn't seem to be listening.

Her mother looked up and spoke with a slur: "Ah, your friend Lautrec. How can you be around the horrid little freak? Just looking at him makes me ill."

"He pays me well, and he has been giving me some drawing lessons," Suzanne replied. "And besides, someday he will be a count and you never know what may happen between us?"

This was news to her mother, and she appeared suddenly more alert. "So the little freak has some nobility. Perhaps, even I should sleep with him," she continued. "Are you sleeping with him?"

"No, but I could. I don't want him to think of me in the same ways as he does all the other women who model for him."

"You mean the other whores," her mother said spitefully. "Just because we model, doesn't make us whores," Suzanne retorted angrily.

"It wasn't the modeling I was talking about," her mother replied with a sly smile on her face. "Perhaps, I will take little Maurice and take in this art exhibit. This Lautrec does know about Maurice?"

"I have told him, but such matters do not seem to interest him," she answered. "And I will be very upset if you ever show up when I am with my friends. It's not my son who shames me."

The older Valadon stood up, obviously annoyed by her daughter's words, but didn't say anything. She wobbled out of the room toward the crying of her grandson.

Suzanne stood up from the table and headed to her bedroom. She perused the dresses she had laid out on the bed and decided on the black one with a tight bodice and a high collar. On her bureau lay her favorite hat. She settled the hat on her head and adjusted it in the mirror.

Misia Godebska sat before the grand piano which took up almost the entire front room of her small flat. She was still dressed in a thick flannel night-shirt, and she wore a pair of knitted wool slippers that her grandmother had sent her from Brussels. The room was cold, and the small coal stove offered little help in warming the room. She scanned the tiny room that housed all of her belongings. The paucity of it all did not bother her for her intuition told her that life was about to flourish.

She was not pleased that she had to cancel her student's lessons this afternoon. Since returning from London, money had been tight, but she had managed to survive with the small income she generated from teaching students who Gabriel Fauré had been sending her. She could not expect much help from her grandparents who provided the money to buy the piano for the flat.

She stroked the smooth mahogany wood of the piano. Fauré had told her that she would need to get an upright piano because a grand would never fit in her small flat. But she insisted on a grand. Her mind drifted to when the piano was first delivered. The deliverymen refused at first to even attempt to carry the piano up the small stairwell into her flat. They were about to leave when her tears softened them, and after four hours of almost completely dismantling the piano, they somehow managed to get the piano inside. She rewarded each of the burly men with a big kiss on the cheek.

Fauré had convinced her that she needed a break from her teaching and to take an afternoon off. Although she was gregarious by nature, six years in a convent school does little for one's social skills. Fauré was taking her to lunch, and according to him, a new exhibition just opened right above the restaurant. He thought she might enjoy seeing the work of some of Paris's young talented artists.

She stroked a few notes on the keyboard and decided to allow herself a day away from the piano. The thought of washing her hair in the frigid air of her apartment was not inviting, but she wanted to look her best. She walked over to the small closet, and realized she had little choice —the red dress or the blue one? She decided on the red dress as the most striking, and she, indeed, wanted to make a big impression.

She poured some cold water into the basin and grabbed some soap for her hair. She caught herself humming a simple song, and realized that she really was looking forward to her day..

Walter Sickert peered out the train window, scanning the French countryside. The morning sun streamed across the vacant fields and he found the sight pleasing. For a moment, he had a desire to paint *en plein air* the next time he visited his mistress in Dieppe. Still, he much preferred the gloom of the interior of a theater, but perhaps painting landscape would be a pleasant diversion.

He looked down at his watch. It was only eight o'clock. He would be in Paris by early afternoon giving him plenty of time to meet Louis Anquetin at the Restaurant du Chalet. He met Anquetin three years earlier when he first came to Paris to see Degas. He felt a strong kinship to Anquetin who like himself had begun painting as recreation but later committed to it as a profession. Anquetin had written him about his new art that he called Synthetism, and Sickert was interested in viewing the new work.

He took out a letter from his leather satchel. It was from James Whistler, his old mentor. Whistler would also be in Paris to do some nocturne painting. He scanned the letter for the name of the hotel where Whistler would be staying and was disappointed not to find it.

"Maybe he will be at Anquetin's exhibition. Jimmy's not one to miss a party," he thought to himself.

After spending a week alone with Roxanne, he craved the company of men. He imagined he loved Roxanne as much as he could love any woman. Sometimes, he thought his handsomeness was a curse for it served as a magnet to women. Their attention flattered him, but he would quickly find them tedious and wish that he were alone. Sex had become a chore for him and left him unsatisfied. He had unfulfilled cravings, but they were not sexual. Across from him sat a woman who smiled at him. She was an attractive woman wearing a fashionable dress and a wide-brimmed hat. She appeared a few years older than him, but after spending a week with the ingénue Roxanne, he found her age appealing. He had noticed her when he first sat down, but he had become occupied with his own thoughts. For a moment he was tempted to engage her in conversation, but he resisted the urge.

He caught his reflection in the train window and muttered to himself, “The curse of the beautiful.”

James Whistler came to Paris to escape London's frigid fall weather and Maude Franklin. He escaped neither. Paris felt even colder than London, and Franklin insisted on joining Whistler. For the moment, he had a respite from both. He sat in one of the luxurious sitting rooms of the hotel Le Meurice sipping a hot cup of coffee. Franklin was feeling poorly and needed more time to rest in their room. He was happy with his solitude.

When in Paris, Le Meurice was his choice of hotel. Although very pricey, painting sales had been excellent, and he was not one to deprive himself of pleasure. The sitting room was almost empty except for a few English businessmen with their wives. Le Meurice used to attract a higher class of clientele, and these were not the kind of people who would recognize him. This morning, he was enjoying his anonymity.

"Monsieur Whistler, a letter has just arrived," a young porter interrupted his quietude.

"Merci," Whistler replied taking the letter from the porter. He recognized the handwriting as that of Walter Sickert, the young man who for a while assisted him with his etchings. He liked Sickert, but he also thought there was something strange and dark about him. Perhaps, that is what he liked about him.

He quickly scanned the contents. Sickert would be in Paris this week before returning to London, and he was hoping that they might get together. He even suggested they might meet at the opening of a new exhibit this afternoon in Montmartre.

He would have enjoyed seeing Sickert and meeting some new Parisian artists, and perhaps best of all, getting away from Maude. Montmartre would be a bit of a trek, and maybe he could convince her that it would tax her strength. As he contemplated the possibility, he was broken out of his reverie by Franklin's voice.

"Jimmie, I'm lonely. You said you would only be gone a few minutes, and it's been over an hour," she whined

He looked up at her. They had been together for over ten years. He remembered her when they first met. She was exciting and vibrant. Now all of that had disappeared. Two pregnancies and a decade of worry had robbed her of vitality. She was still attractive, but in a more matronly way. Her long flowing red hair had darkened, and she had cut it short.

"I didn't want to disturb your rest," he lied. "And I just received a letter from Walter Sickert about a new exhibition that just opened in Paris. You remember Sickert. He was the young man who helped me with my etchings."

"Yes, vaguely," she replied. Sickert's image flashed through her mind. He was a tall handsome man, who fawned embarrassingly over Whistler. She remembered little else, but his memory evoked some unexplained dislike.

"The exhibition is in Montmartre, and I thought I might make an afternoon of it while you rested," he continued.

She glared down at him. "You'll find any excuse to get away from me. First, it was Paris so that you could do some painting, and we've been here a week and you haven't painted a single moment. So if you're going to this exhibition, I'm going with you."

"Montmartre is quite a ways from here. And you're right. I need to do some work. I have been thinking about a new series of nocturnes right here in Paris." Whistler attempted to placate her. He never hesitated confronting his enemies, but not his lovers.

"I'll be right up to the room after I finish my coffee," he said.

"I'll be waiting," she said, still angry.

He watched her as she stormed off. He would have enjoyed the exhibition, but not with her at his side.

Afternoon

Van Gogh was still angry at his brother. Theo had never arrived for their lunch date, and he had just enough francs to cover his lunch. The show had added stress to their already tenuous relationship. They argued violently last night as they were hanging the show, and Theo left around midnight leaving him alone to finish hanging. He hated that he had to rely on his brother for his survival.

"Perhaps this show will generate some sales," he thought out loud. He had come to Paris last year to salvage his life as an artist. In the past year, he had painted hundreds of pieces, but sales had been sparse. If it weren't for Theo putting pressure on his art clients, sales would be nonexistent. For a moment, he questioned whether even those sales were real, but he quickly dismissed the thought. One of the reasons he organized the show was to prove to himself that he could sell his own work, and not depend on Theo.

As he reached the top of the stairs to the ballroom entrance, he was swept with immense pleasure viewing the large room filled with art. Despite the day's thick clouds, the large skylights lit the room well. One of the real advantages of doing your own show, you have control of the art —you can show what you want and where you want.

His work dominated the room beginning with a large panoramic view of Montmartre which he had completed last year, and it was his most impressionistic piece in the show. The remainder of the pieces were pictures he had painted the past summer. There were a couple of cafe scenes, several still lifes, a large nude and a small self-portrait.

He scanned the room to see if any of the artists had arrived, but there were only a few of the restaurant's customers browsing the work. By their dress, he could tell they were workmen on lunch break. He had the immediate impulse to bring them over to view his work, but what was the point—workmen don't buy art.

Two men brushed past him. They were shaking their heads in disdain as they passed him. "What did these clods know anyway," he thought to himself. He liked having the room to himself so he could stroll the exhibit without being disturbed, but he glanced back to see if Theo or any of the artists had arrived.

He stopped before the wall he devoted to the work of Anquetin and Bernard. He had mixed feelings about the paintings. He appreciated their bold use of color, but there was no character in their stroke. He had imagined a much larger exhibition with paintings from Seurat and Signac, but they refused to show because of their rift with Anquetin and Bernard.

"No matter, more room to show my own," he muttered.

He continued on to Lautrec's wall. All of the paintings were informal portraits of women. He recognized Marie Valadon as the model for two of the pieces. She had never modeled in Cormon's studio so he had never painted her. He rarely painted nudes—not because of the subject but because he rarely had the money to pay the model. He liked Lautrec's work, especially his use of stroke, and the soft impressionist strokes stood out against the brash color of Anquetin's and Bernard's pieces.

He heard someone enter the room, and he turned to see Theo approaching. Theo showed a disconsolate expression as he neared him.

"Vincent, I'm sorry about last night. I was tired from the late evening," Theo said awkwardly hugging his brother.

Vincent said nothing in the embrace, and he wondered how he could ever be so angry at this loving brother. He also thought of asking Theo for the money he spent on lunch, but he decided to keep quiet.

* * *

Louis Anquetin knew by Sickert's expression that he was not impressed by his paintings. There was that long, silent pause when someone is attempting to find something positive to say and nothing comes to mind.

"You certainly aren't afraid to push your color. I can see you've moved on to a new direction since the paintings from Breton," Sickert broke the silence.

For a moment, Anquetin was tempted to defend the

painting, and explain the theory that underlaying the work. Sickert was a tonalist, and nothing that he could say would move him from that aesthetic.

"Emile and I believe that Impressionism is at a dead-end. Cezanne was the first to recognize this, and he has moved beyond Impressionism. And we think we have moved beyond Cezanne," Anquetin explained.

In the crowded room, the two men stood out. They were both tall, well over six feet, and both were handsome men in their late twenties. However, except for their height and age, they were disparate in appearance. Sickert was the refined Teutonic with light blond hair, clean-shaven with delicate features. He originally sought a career on the stage, but his acting never matched his looks, and he had recently embarked on the serious career as a painter. Anquetin was Latin with thick black hair and the beginnings of a full beard that covered his bulbous face. He too had flirted with other careers before gravitating to painting.

The awkward silence resumed. The attention of both men was directed elsewhere, but they were anchored there. Anquetin scanned the room intently, and caught sight of Paul Gauguin entering the exhibit.

"Walter, I see an old friend. I hope you will excuse me," Anquetin said without trying to hide the relief in his voice.

"Certainly, I haven't had a chance to meet that Lautrec fellow. He looks like a bit of character. Perhaps, I will see you in Breton this summer?" Sickert responded as both headed off in different directions.

* * *

Lautrec enjoyed his chat with Sickert, who seemed to appreciate his work. Lautrec was something of an Anglophile, and enjoyed the opportunity to practice his English. The conversation closed with an invitation to visit Sickert next spring in London.

Lautrec was concerned. He had expected to see his father, and it was after three o'clock, and the afternoon light had already begun to fade. Although his father had been living in Paris for a few months, they had not visited once since he arrived. Many promises had been made, but none had been kept. Disappointment had just begun to creep over him when he spied his father entering the hall.

Count Alfonse Lautrec approached his son with a bearing fitting one of the noble class. He maintained a full beard that seemed to explode off of his face. Beneath his wild mane, he and his son shared many features. Henri inherited his father's wide arching eyebrows and bulbous nose with an abbreviated chin. He carried himself with a pompous expression of self-importance. Henri smiled at his father as much out of amusement for his father's exaggerated sense of self-importance as his genuine pleasure at seeing him.

Even without the deformity of his legs, Henri would not have approached his father's height. Despite being drummed out of the French cavalry after only a few years, his father presented himself with the demeanor of a military man. The elder Lautrec had little ambition himself and believed that work was beneath his social stature. He allowed his son to embark on his art career as much out of lack of concern than any enthusiastic support for the choice. Although he did not understand why his son would pursue a life that depended on sales to the bourgeoisie, he would allow it so long that he did not embarrass the family or himself.

His father's presence in Henri's life had diminished as Henri grew older, which made Henri pursue his father's approval with greater fervor. His father was something of an amateur artist himself, and Henri claimed that his artistic talent came from his father's side of the family.

"Papa, I was afraid you were not going to make it," Lautrec said honestly.

"My driver dropped me off at the wrong place, and I've spent the last hour wandering up and down these confounded Montmartre hills. No one seems to know about this exhibition. I would have hoped to see your work in an actual gallery, not in the attic of a workmen's restaurant," he said, not shielding his son from any of his bitterness.

"I'm sorry Papa, but this is the only place that Van Gogh could secure," Henri apologized.

"So that Van Gogh fellow organized this. I would have hoped that he would be a better organizer than an artist. I saw his work when I first came in. I can't believe that anyone would actually buy the work. It looks like the efforts of a spastic ten-year-old."

Lautrec was beginning to wish he had not invited his father.

"So these are your paintings," the elder Lautrec said as he scanned the paintings on the wall.

"Are these women some of your whores?" He asked.

"No, they are some of the women who model in my studio," Henri replied. "Well they look like whores," his father continued. "So who do you think will buy these paintings? What would your mother say if I brought one of these for her? Henri, we didn't allow you to come to Paris to paint whores."

"I didn't remember you ever being around to allow me to do anything," Henri answered letting his anger show. "

You know I can stop your allowance anytime I wish," his father said in a threatening tone.

"You mean that pittance you call an allowance. I could barely live on that whether I painted or not."

"Don't test me son or we'll see how well you live on your art sales."

"Look Henri," his father's voice softened. "You'll need to paint the kind of things that will get you into the Salon. If I were you, I'd probably paint whores as well, but I have no ambitions to succeed as an artist."

Lautrec's own anger subsided with a slight hint of kindness from his father.

"I know I can't make you like my art, but none of my paintings, no matter how much I try, will never find their way into the Salon. If I'm going to make it as an artist, I'll have to do it my way, and not according to the dictates of a bunch of old men who have not created anything new in the last two centuries."

"Well the choice is yours. We had hoped you would have chosen a nobler path with your art, but you are going to have live with your own decisions. But remember, when you sign your paintings with the family name, it reflects on us as well."

"I wouldn't want to paint anything that would embarrass the family," Lautrec replied, concealing his sarcasm.

"That's the spirit," his father answered apparently oblivious to the sarcasm. "In your next exhibit, I'm certain there will be work that will make us proud."

The elder Lautrec took out his pocket watch as though he was missing an appointment.

"I haven't had lunch; would you like to join me?" He asked his son.

"I'm sorry Papa, but we all promised Van Gogh that we would stay the full afternoon. We are all getting together at my studio after the show. Perhaps, you could join us?"

"I'm sorry Henri. I need to be on my way, and I suspect I would not fit in very well with your friends."

"Well, we need to have dinner soon," Henri said as his father turned to leave.

"Yes we must do that," his father replied.

His father walked a few steps and turned once more to his son. "I'm sorry I missed your birthday. I shall have a nice gift for you when we have dinner."

"Thank you, Papa," Lautrec replied, watching his father scurry down the hall.

* * *

"Father troubles?"

Lautrec turned to discover a young woman smiling at him.

"I know the feeling. I have a father who wants me to be something I'm not or maybe he just wants me to be nothing. In either case, we're better off without them," she continued.

Lautrec had never seen her before. She was tall with her hair pushed up into a bun that accentuated her height even more. She wore a bright red dress with a low-cut neckline displaying an ample cleavage. Long full eyebrows curved over her wide-set dark brown eyes. She had a full face with a pert nose and small delicate lips. At that moment, Lautrec thought she was the most beautiful woman he had ever seen.

"I see you enjoy painting women," the young girl observed motioning toward the two pieces on the wall. "Is she your lover?" The question caught Lautrec off guard.

"Yes, I do enjoy painting women," he replied somewhat flustered. "She is one of my models, nothing more."

"Humm," she murmured, returning her attention to the paintings. "I think she is more than just a model. These are too sensitive for just a model. If she is not your lover, you certainly would wish she were."

"You seem to know a great deal about life for being such a young person," he said looking squarely in her eyes.

"You seem to know a great deal about life for being such a young person," she laughed, returning his stare.

Lautrec smiled, enjoying the conversation.

"Perhaps, someday you will paint my portrait," she said, pushing back some imaginary stray hairs from the side of her face.

"Only if you will be my lover," Lautrec responded, half seriously.

"I don't think that will ever be the case. Monsieur. . . ?"

"I am Henri Toulouse-Lautrec and will someday be Count Toulouse-Lautrec."

"Ahh, a noble painter, I see," she laughed again.

"Well, Monsieur Toulouse-Lautrec you are a talented painter. And I think one day you will paint my portrait, but we will never be lovers," she said extending her hand to be kissed. Lautrec responded with a kiss that lingered.

"I see my friend is about ready to leave," she said looking toward an older man who was waving to her. "It has been a pleasure to meet you, Henri."

"The pleasure has been mine as well. And your name, mademoiselle?"

"Misia. . . Misia Godebska," she said, waving goodbye.

Lautrec watched as the young woman reached the older man. She placed her hand into his waiting arm, and Lautrec could tell she was recounting their conversation with him.

"Who was that woman with Fauré?" Emile Bernard asked, rushing toward Lautrec. "She is quite stunning."

"Her name is Misia Godebska, and I would quite agree that she is quite stunning," Lautrec answered.

"She must be one of Fauré's new protégés. I am told that he sleeps with all of them," Bernard mused. "I don't think he will be sleeping with this one; nor do I think she will be his protégé for long," Lautrec said, as they both watched her leave.

* * *

Vincent Van Gogh stood in front of a long wall of his paintings. His brother Theo had left, and the exhibition hall had emptied of most of the visitors. He was disappointed that there had been no sales for his work. Theo had told him that one of the collectors had expressed interest in one of the still lifes, but he was always suspicious of Theo's veracity concerning the interest and intent of collectors.

The sales disappointment and his poor night's sleep began to overtake him. His weariness was coupled with hunger, and he did not have the energy or the francs for dinner. He thought about the after-show party at Lautrec's. He hated these gatherings where his faulty French often failed him and he felt like an outsider. There would be little food, but much to drink. He did not have the energy for this as well, but the prospect of returning to his cold flat alone was even more depressing. As he was pondering his choices, he could see Anquetin approaching him with another man. He was a man about his age. He was handsome with a small mustache and a well-groomed goatee. He walked with a confident cosmopolitan air, but he did not look well.

"Vincent, I'd like to introduce you to Paul Gauguin. Paul is a painter whom I met last summer in Brittany. He very much liked your work, and wanted to meet the artist," Anquetin said presenting Gauguin.

"It is a pleasure," Van Gogh replied extending his hand toward the stranger.

"The pleasure is all mine," Gauguin replied eagerly

shaking his hand.

"It is a pleasure," Van Gogh replied extending his hand toward the stranger.

"The pleasure is all mine," Gauguin replied eagerly shaking his hand.

"I think your work is powerful, and it makes me want to rush back to my easel," Gauguin continued.

"I appreciate your compliments. I only wish the collectors shared your enthusiasm," Van Gogh replied, sensing a kinship with this man.

"What do collectors know? They only buy what the critics tell them to buy. Your work is too fresh and innovative for those people. Unfortunately, I am currently in an extremely awkward financial state or I would have bought any one of several pieces."

"I can certainly relate to such a condition," Van Gogh replied. "But I would be honored if you would allow me to take you to dinner. I certainly can find the francs for that," Gauguin offered. "But first, why don't you show me around this exhibit? I understand you called your exhibition, *Expressionists of Les Petits Boulevards*. You must tell me how you came up with this?" Gauguin asked, gently, patting Van Gogh on the back.

Anquetin stood awkwardly in ignored silence as he watched the two men leave without a word of goodbye. He was about to join Lautrec, but paused after seeing Sickert approaching Lautrec.

* * *

Walter Sickert was disappointed that James Whistler had not appeared at the exhibit. He was looking forward to an evening of conversation with his old mentor. He decided to ask Lautrec to accompany him for dinner.

"Yes, I would enjoy that very much," Lautrec said, accepting the invitation. "We are all returning to my studio later this evening, and I hope you can join us."

"That would be nice. I was dreading the idea of spending my first night in Paris alone," Sickert replied.

"I suspect you do not spend many nights alone," Lautrec laughed at the man who towered over him.

"And, you as well," Sickert said turning his attention to Lautrec's work. "You seem to favor this model," Sickert said pointing to a painting of a pensive young woman sitting alone with a bottle of wine, staring into space.

"That's Suxanne Valadon. She models for many of the artists of Montmartre, and she is something of a friend."

"Something. . .," Sickert mused.

"Yes, we're not lovers, and I help her with her drawings from time to time," Lautrec continued.

"So she's an artist as well," Sickert returned his attention to the image on the canvas.

"Perhaps she will be someday."

"My ears are burning. I think I am being spoken of." Both men turned to see a young woman approaching. She was a woman with long arching eyebrows over dark brown eyes, almost black. Her face was ovate with sensual lips, and although she was smiling, her eyes revealed a serious, almostsad expression. Her thick black hair, parted in the middle, was worn up adding to her impression of height. She wore a high-neck black dress that fitted tightly around her waist and bodice accentuating her voluptuousness.

She rushed up to Lautrec and to kissed him on the cheek.

"And who may this gentleman be," Valadon asked with a flirtatious smile directed at Sickert.

"Walter, may I present the queen of Montmartre, Suzanne Valadon," Lautrec said with a grand gesture.

"It is my pleasure," Sickert replied, kissing Valadon's hand.

"Well, perhaps, it will be," Valadon replied with a slight laugh.

"Henri tells me you are an excellent model. Perhaps, you may model for me while I am in Paris."

"Ahh, you are a painter as well. I thought you may be one of Henri's actor friends."

"That was in another life," Sickert replied. "But now painting is my life."

Valadon continued to focus her attention on Sickert. "It seems to be everyone's."

"I understand you are an artist as well." Sickert continued.

"I only dabble in an occasional drawing or two. Henri is the true artist here. I am much too intimidated by his work."
"So you may model for me?" Sickert persisted.

"Well, I only take off my clothes for the great ones. Are you such an artist?" Valadon asked with her tone becoming more serious.

" I hope to be someday."

"Well then someday, perhaps I will model for you,"

Evening

Lautrec's studio had gradually emptied with only a few of the artists and Suzanne Valadon remaining. Lautrec was drunk and stood unsteadily next to Valadon at the bar covered with empty bottles and dirty glasses. Lautrec whispered something in Valadon's ear making her laugh bawdily.

Anquetin and Sickert stood in front of a Lautrec easel viewing a half-finished painting. Their words became louder in some obvious disagreement. Van Gogh and Gauguin were sitting together on a small sofa in the corner. Their conversation was animate and friendly.

"My friends," Lautrec began, loudly tapping a spoon on the side of a glass, "I want to thank you for coming to celebrate my birthday and our wonderful exhibition. We didn't sell much, but it was my great honor to show with such a talented group of painters. I hope you enjoyed my earthquakes, but I'm afraid the absinthe is all gone (motioning to the empty bottles on the bar top) and perhaps I am as well."

Lautrec collapsed back on the chair and would have surely fallen off if he had not been steadied by Valadon. His words seemed to make little impression on his guests who continued with their own conversations.

"Frankly, sir, I see no subtlety in this new work of yours. It looks more like the kind of montage that I did in kindergarten." Sickert's words were disparaging, but they were spoken in a dispassionate tone.

Unlike his composed antagonist, Anquetin's face grew red, and looked as though it would burst. His fists were clenched, and it appeared that he was about to strike Sickert.

"Your ideas are nothing more than trite ramblings of someone who can't escape the past. It is a fault of you personally and your race collectively. Nothing new has come out of your island in the past three hundred years. Paris is the center of the art world, and the only decent artists in London are the Americans, who could not succeed in their own country."

Sickert's voice was still calm, but it belied the anger in his eyes. "I should hope we do not necessarily equate new with good. If you closed your eyes and squirted a hundred tubes of paint on a canvas, you would probably call that avant-garde as well. Novelty is the last refuge of the untalented, and I do find your work novel."

Sickert's words exasperated Anquetin even more. If he didn't leave then, blows might have been exchanged. He grabbed his hat, and looked over to Lautrec. “Henri, I don’t know what you like about these Brits, but I didn’t come here to be belittled by someone with so little talent.” With that, Anquetin stormed out of the studio.

The outburst silenced the room. But after a few moments, Sickert joined Lautrec and Valadon while Gauguin and Van Gogh resumed their conversation.

“I’m afraid I’ve stayed much longer than I had anticipated,” Gauguin said. “I’ve enjoyed meeting you and look forward to visiting your studio.”

Gauguin stood wobbly and shook hands with Van Gogh. He staggered toward the door and would have fallen if Van Gogh had not rushed to his aid. “I afraid I’m in no condition to go anywhere,” Gauguin said, collapsing into Van Gogh’s arms, who guided him back to the sofa.

“Henri, you don’t have a blanket I can cover him with,” Van Gogh asked Lautrec. “I’ll find you one,” Valadon called back.

Valadon returned with a blanket and handed it to Van Gogh, who gently covered the unconscious Gauguin on the sofa.

“Give Henri my thanks for the evening,” Van Gogh said, who suddenly found himself surprisingly sober. He left without bothering to say goodbye.

Valadon turned to discover that Lautrec had also passed out with his body draped over the bar. The only sound in the room was Lautrec’s loud snuffling in his sleep. She found herself uncomfortably alone with Sickert, who was leering at her. He approached her with the same leer on his face.

"My hotel is only a few blocks away. Perhaps, you would like to join me," Sickert propositioned her.

Valadon was accustomed to such propositions from artists, but there was something about his tone that alarmed her.

"I don't know what kind of woman you believe me to be, but I never sleep with anyone who I have just met. I will just get another blanket and stay here with Henri." She hoped that mentioning Lautrec would drive Sickert away.

"Suit yourself, but my bed will certainly be much more comfortable than sleeping on the floor here," Sickert said.

"I will be fine," she said moving over to the other side of the studio. She thought about waking Lautrec, but she could tell by his deep snuffling that it would be hopeless.

Instead of leaving, Sickert opened the cupboard above the bar to find a half-finished bottle of cognac. He poured a large glass and slouched himself down on a chair with his attention still directed toward Valadon in the corner.

His presence made her nervous, but her weariness overcame her, and she fell asleep.

* * *

For a moment, Suzanne Valadon thought she was dreaming. She awoke to find Sickert on top of her. Her dress was pulled up to her neck, and she could feel his hand tugging at her underwear. She tried to scream, but Sickert muffled it with his hand across her mouth. She gazed frantically around the room hoping for rescue, but the only sounds to be heard in the darkness was Sickert's panting.

She thought of succumbing to his attack, but her fear was turning to anger. She let her body go limp, and she could feel Sickert's grip loosen. At that instant, she flailed her free hand across Sickert's face with her fingernails ripping into his skin. He howled in pain and clutched his face. Before he could grab her again, she rammed her knee into his groin andhe rolled over on his side. She sprung to her feet before he could react.

"You filthy pig," she screamed looking back as she reached the door. Her screams failed to awaken either Lautrec or Gauguin, and she slammed the door behind her.

Valadon's mind was racing as she approached the street. It was still dark, but a faint glow in the east suggested an approaching sunrise. The stupor from last night's bout of drinking had vanished and her mind was clear. She thought of going to the police to report Sickert's assault, but how seriously would police treat such a report from a model in Montmartre?

For a moment, she thought of returning to Lautrec's confronting Sickert in front of Lautrec and Gauguin, but her fear was stronger than her anger. It was cold, and she was only wearing her dress. It would be a long walk to her apartment, and at this time of night, there would be no carriages for hire. She just wanted to get home and put the night behind her. She placed her hands under her armpits to warm them and began the long trek home.

A wet fog gradually enveloped her, adding to the chill of the evening. There was an eerie silence in the night. It was a

Paris to which she was unaccustomed—so quiet, so still. She might have enjoyed the moment if it weren't for the cold that penetrated her body and made her shiver.

The sound of her cadenced steps lulled her into a mindless reverie. She gradually began to be aware of a second set of steps far behind her. Numbed by the cold, their sound did not immediately register. Then, suddenly she was swept with fear when she turned around and saw in the darkness a tall figure looming in the fog a half-block away. She wanted to believe that it was her imagination or at least that it was someone other than Sickert, but she knew that wasn't the case.

She turned around again and quickened her pace as the figure drew closer.

When Sickert left Lautrec's, he was furious, but that fury had changed into some new unexperienced emotion. He had followed Valadon for several blocks without knowing what he intended to do when he caught up with her. He fingered the kitchen knife he had grabbed almost unconsciously when he left the apartment. Now as he got closer, he realized that he was stalking her, and this helpless figure had become his prey. This feeling gave him palpable pleasure, and he slowed down because he wanted to prolong these sensations.

Her body was no longer a sexual object. He had no desire to experience her in that way. His lust was much deeper and more profound than that. He could imagine the fear in her eyes when he snared her, and how that fear would grow when she saw the blade. Then he imagined the blood. The sensation swept him beyond any lust he had ever felt. "I will bathe in her blood," were the words he spoke to himself. He could tell by her pace that she had spotted him, and he knew it was time. He could see in the predawn dusk that the hunt had brought them to a cemetery. It was as though fate had found the perfect spot for the kill.

Valadon tried to run. Even with her fear, the cold had deprived her body of the energy to flee. She looked around for a place to hide and thought maybe she could conceal herself behind one of the large grave sculptures that dotted the cemetery beside her. But the fog had already begun to lift, and the darkness had turned to gray. There was no hope.

Sickert could feel his blood racing as he approached the entrance to the cemetery. His eyes scanned the graveyard for his prey, but within the shadows, he felt the presence of another. Before he could react, he heard the words, "Is that you Walter?"

Sickert turned to discover James Whistler standing by his easel with a small lamp. Whistler's voice deflated his mania and he was overcome by a profound disconsolation. In his periphery, he could see Valadon sneaking off into the cemetery. He looked over to Whistler, who was smiling broadly beneath his famous mustache. He approached his old friend and noticed a half-finished nocturne on his easel.

"Hello Jimmy," Sickert said quietly.

Epilogue

Walter Sickert would return to London in 1888. Shortly thereafter, eleven women were murdered in the working-class London neighborhood of Whitechapel, an area frequently by Sickert. Five of the murders were attributed to Jack the Ripper. The identity of the Ripper has never been solved, but Sickert has often been mentioned as a prominent suspect.

In just fifteen years after *Les Impressionists*, Van Gogh, Lautrec, Gauguin and Whistler would be dead. Bernard and Anquetin would disavow their allegiance to modernist painting, and return to more classical leanings. They both turned to teaching and writing and died in relative obscurity. Shortly after *Les Petits*, Suzanne Valadon begins to paint seriously and assumes the Synthetist style of Anquetin and Bernard. In 1911, her first major show in Paris established her as a major artist, becoming the first woman to show at the Société Nationale des Beaux-Arts. She paints continually until her death in 1938. Walter Sickert dies four years later in 1942, and is recognized as one of Britain's finest impressionists. Misia Sert marries three times and reign over Paris's artistic community for over four decades. She dies in 1950, the last of *The Impressionists of the Petits Boulevards* players.

www.ingramcontent.com/pod-product-compliance
Lightning Source LLC
LaVergne TN
LVHW020644100826
845148LV00012B/2339

* 9 7 8 1 7 3 2 6 4 9 1 4 9 *